Happy Birth Day

by Jane Sorenson

illustrated by Kathleen L. Smith

STANDARD PUBLISHING
Cincinnati, Ohio   24-02938

LIBRARY OF CONGRESS
Library of Congress Cataloging-in-Publication Data

Sorenson, Jane.
  Happy birth day/by Jane Sorenson; illustrated by Kathleen Smith.
      p. cm. – (A Katie Hooper book; 3)
      Summary: Katie and her family move into their new home just in time for the arrival of a new baby sister.
      ISBN 0-87403-488-4
      [1. Family life – Fiction. 2. Moving, Household – Fiction. 3. Babies – Fiction. 4. Christian life – Fiction.] I. Smith, Kathleen, 1950- ill. II. Title. III. Title: Happy birthday. IV. Series: Sorenson, Jane. Katie Hooper book; 3.
  PZ7.S7214Hap 1988
  [Fic] – dc19   88-6399
                                                                CIP
                                                                AC

With all my love,
to Thalia McDonald,

whose love for God's little children
burns brighter than life itself!

A Note from the Author

Dear Reader:

It's time for the long-awaited birth of the Hoopers' baby! The Hoopers are fortunate, indeed, that it takes place in Penrose Community Hospital's new Birth Center! This story and the characters are, of course, fiction. Although the hospital was generous in providing both a tour and follow-up support, it is in no way responsible for what I have written.

Readers should remember that "rules" in hospitals throughout the United States vary a great deal. Practices permitted in Colorado Springs may not be followed in your community.

Also, I wish to tell you that the factual information about God's miracle called birth was gleaned from a book called *The Miracle of Growth*, published by the University of Illinois Press at Urbana, 1950. The book is a written account of the popular exhibit at Chicago's Museum of Science and Industry.

Writing a book about this miracle has been almost as awe-inspiring and exciting as the birth of a "real" baby. I repeat, *almost!*

Jane Sorenson

A Glance Back

"There," said Harry Upjohn, as he knotted the rope one last time, "I think that will hold." He stepped back from the big yellow truck and grinned. "OK, kids?"

I grinned back and nodded. Frankly, I've never been great at knots.

"It looks OK to me," Jason said.

"Harry, we never could have moved without you," my father said.

"That's what it's all about—helping our Christian brothers and sisters!" Mr. Upjohn said. His bald head shone in the Colorado sunlight.

Mom smiled. "I'm glad we're part of God's family! Our other relatives are scattered all over the country."

"Well," Mr. Upjohn said, "unless there's something more I can do here, I'll start down to Woodland Park. Maybe we can even get your things unloaded before supper time."

"We'll be right behind you," Dad said. "We just need one last look around the cabin."

My family watched and waved as the truck eased its way down the lane. Then Mom threw her arms around Dad. "Steve, we've made it! We're going to be all moved before the baby comes! It's a miracle!"

Jason turned to me. He's my older brother. "We aren't done yet," he muttered. "It will take weeks to get settled at the other house."

I was glad our parents hadn't heard him. "They know that," I told him. "Please try not to be so negative!"

Mom and Dad finally remembered we were here. "OK, everybody. Time for one last goodbye to the cabin," Dad said.

"But Mayblossom McDuff said we could come back to visit any time," I reminded him. She's the new owner of the cabin.

It won't ever be the same, Katie," Jason said.

Just as I started to protest, Mom nodded. "I'm afraid Jason's right," she said.

Silently, I turned and walked through the open cabin door. I nearly stepped on January, my stupid dog. He was lying stretched out in the sunlight in front of the fireplace. He opened one eye, looked at me, and slowly stood up.

"Time to say good-bye," I told him. "From now on, we'll be living in Home Sweet Home."

Probably it was my imagination, but January looked like he was nodding. He walked over and rubbed his head against my leg. And when I leaned down to rub his fur, he looked up at me with the cutest expression on his face.

I glanced around. Without our furniture, the living room looked big and plain and cold. I remembered the day a few weeks ago when we found out the cabin was being sold. And the next thing we knew, our home had been purchased by a vacationing author from the East!

I'll be honest. When your father paints mountains for a living, you never have much money! So finding another home wasn't easy. By the time we finally saw the old wreck of a place near Woodland Park, we were even thankful!

For the past several weeks, all of us have worked hard to fix up the old house. But, although we call it Home Sweet Home, so far it's been more of an adventure than a home!

I started climbing the ladder to my room in the loft. It's the only room I've ever had. My parents lived in this cabin when I was born. In fact, they even lived here when Jason was born. And he's going into eighth grade!

"Look, Katie!" Jason called. "January's following you!"

I couldn't believe it! Ever since I got that dog, I've been trying to teach him to climb the ladder! But the only way I could get him up to my room was to carry him.

"I always thought he could do it," I laughed. I waited while January awkwardly made his way to the top. "Good dog!" I said. "I'm proud of you!" He followed me into my room.

Except for a dirty white sock and mountains of dust balls, my room was empty. Frankly—this is the neatest my room's ever been! But across one paneled wall marched a row of pencil drawings. Each sketch showed the face of the same person—me, Katie Hooper!

"Oh, no!" I said. "It's a good thing I came back up! I forgot to bring my pictures!"

Every year, on my birthday, my father sketches my picture. Dad drew the first one the day I was born. It shows a bright-eyed little baby with no hair!

In the second sketch, I have teeth—but still not much hair. I am wearing a tiny bow somebody tied onto a few hairs on the top of my head!

In every picture, I am smiling. Mom says they really should have named me Joy! In the seventh sketch, my front teeth are gone again, and I'm smiling a big toothless grin! But from then on, the pictures look more and more like Katie Hooper!

Jason stuck his head in my door. "So this is what your room looks like! I always wondered!" He grinned. Frankly, my brother keeps his room so neat it's sickening! "We'd better get going," he said. "Mr. Upjohn will be waiting for us."

"I forgot to take my sketches," I told him. "I was afraid they'd get wrecked, so I saved them until last. And then I nearly left them."

"I'll help you," Jason said.

"Thanks! I can do it," I said. "But it would help if you'd take January down."

"Suit yourself." My brother picked up the dog, turned, and left.

I don't know why, but Dad has never sketched Jason on his birthdays. So, naturally, that kind of makes my pictures even more special! I really don't know the reason why. I used to imagine it was because Dad liked me best! But, of course, I know that isn't true.

Now, one by one, I took down my drawings and started to leave. At the door, I turned and looked back one last time.

Suddenly, my room no longer looked liked my room at all! It could have belonged to absolutely anybody! I glanced at the dust balls and grinned. Well, it could never be Jason's room, but almost anyone else's!

Climbing down the ladder with my pictures in one hand wasn't easy. When I got to the bottom, my family was nowhere in sight. Looking out the window, I spotted Jason sitting in Purple Jeep with January. That figured. I don't think my brother was ever a minute late in his life!

And then I heard my parents talking in their bedroom.

"It's been a good life here, hasn't it?" Dad asked. "Elizabeth, you aren't sorry you left your family to come with me to Colorado?"

"Of course not, Steve!" Mom said. "I wanted to share your life and your dreams! And the Lord has blessed us beyond anything I could have imagined!"

"When He provided this cabin, it was such a wonderful surprise!" Dad said. "But I guess I thought we'd live here forever!"

"Maybe the Lord knew we'd be crowded here," Mom said. "With the new baby, I mean."

"That's true," Dad said. "The baby really will change everything! I only wish the next place were nicer. Frankly, I hate having you move into such a mess!"

"The house will be fine, Steve," Mom said. "I'm just thankful we'll be there before I have to go to the hospital."

"I guess we'd better round up the kids and get started," Dad said.

"Good-bye little dream cabin!" Mom said.

"Good-bye little piece of Heaven!" Dad said. "Hey, Elizabeth, you're crying!"

"I'll be OK," Mom said. "I suddenly realized that this is the end of the first chapter of our family life!"

"I love you, Elizabeth!" Dad said. "Shall we turn the page to see what's written in the next chapter?"

"I'm ready!" Mom said.

Hand-in-hand my parents walked out into the living room. I could tell they were surprised to see me.

"I heard what you said," I told them. "I couldn't help listening!"

"It's OK, Katie," Dad said. "It's no secret."

With her free hand, Mom reached up and wiped a tear from her eye. Then she took hold of my hand. "Come on, Katie," she smiled. "Let's find out what happens next!"

A Surprise Party

As we pulled away in Purple Jeep, nobody said a word. Even Mom was strangely quiet.

I looked back until I could no longer see the log cabin. Our life there had been so good! I remembered family treasure hunts, and nature walks, and reading out loud by the fire. The kids at school can't believe we've never had a television. But, frankly, we haven't even missed it!

Suddenly, Jason spoke. "We'll have to come back up sometime to clean the cabin."

"Jason, sometimes you are impossible!" I said. "Who put you in charge of our lives?"

"Somebody has to be responsible," he said.

January opened his eyes, snorted, and went back to sleep.

14

The drive down the mountain went fast. By the time Dad turned onto our road, I was really getting excited. Maybe Sara would be waiting for me! Sara's my new friend.

"What in the world!" Dad said.

As we neared the old Victorian house, the side of the road was jammed with cars and pickup trucks. And then we saw that our front yard was full of people!

"What's going on?" Jason asked. "It looks like somebody's having a party!"

"Surprise!" yelled Harry Upjohn. "Welcome to Woodland Park!"

"I can't believe it!" Dad said.

I opened my door and climbed down carefully to keep from messing up my sketches. Dad came around to help Mom get down.

"You must be Elizabeth!" A smiling woman with pure white hair stepped forward and hugged Mom. "I'm Marty Upjohn."

"Hi, Marty," Mom said. "What's happening?"

"We're here to help you!" she said. Then she laughed. "The truth is, our Sunday-school class has a party every chance we get!"

While we stood there, Mr. Upjohn waved his arm toward the yellow truck. "Let's go, you guys!" he yelled. "You can introduce yourselves to Steve while we unload the furniture."

I was overwhelmed. While lots of women

15

stepped up to meet Mom, I just stood there watching and hanging onto my drawings. Mom noticed and turned toward me. "This is our daughter, Katie," she said.

"Welcome, Katie!" When Mrs. Upjohn smiled, the corners of her eyes crinkled. "What grade will you be in?"

When I told her, she said, "Oh, good! Our granddaughter, Laura, is your age!"

I felt excited. "Does Laura go to school in Woodland Park? What's her last name?" I asked.

"Laura Logan. Do you know her?"

"I know who she is," I said. "Is she here?" I hadn't noticed any kids.

"The young people are having their own party," she explained.

"Hi, Katie!" A redheaded girl slipped through the crowd and stood there grinning.

"Hi, Sara!" I grinned, too. "I was hoping I'd see you."

"I had this weird idea that I'd come over and welcome you," she said. "I thought you said you didn't know anybody in Woodland Park!"

"We don't," I said softly, so nobody would hear me. "Except for a few kids at school. To be honest, I've never seen these people before in my entire life!"

"Oh, come on!" Sara said.

"It's the truth!"

16

By now two men were carrying our kitchen table toward the house.

"Can you come here, Elizabeth?" Dad called. "We need you to tell us where to put things!"

"They look just like ants!" Sara said, as we watched everybody hurrying around.

I was tired of holding onto my pictures. "Want to go up and see my room?" I asked.

We ran across the yard and through the back door. It was hard to keep from running into somebody! While the men carried things in, some of the women were opening boxes and organizing the kitchen. Things were quieter upstairs.

"Well, here it is," I said.

"It's a yucky color," Sara said. "I would think you'd want to paint the walls."

"I do," I said. "But we ran out of time. We wanted to get moved before Mom goes to the hospital to have the baby." I put the sketches on the corner of my desk.

"Out of the way, girls," my father called. "Here comes your bed, Katie! Where shall we put it?"

I had to think fast. I pointed to the far wall.

"I'll help you make the bed," Sara offered. "Then tonight you'll be all set."

I couldn't believe how fast the truck was unloaded! At that point, everyone assembled on the porch for a cold drink.

"I don't know how to thank you," my father told the people. "Nothing like this has ever happened to us before!"

"Harry figured you could use a little help, what with the baby coming and all," a man said.

"We were hoping he could get you to move on a Saturday!" another man said.

Dad laughed. "I wondered why he kept insisting we reserve the truck for today!"

"We have a fellowship supper every month anyway," Mrs. Upjohn explained. "I hope you won't mind that we invited ourselves over!"

"You mean you brought food?" Mom asked.

Everybody laughed.

"We even brought folding tables from the church!" Mr. Upjohn said. "Could we set them up in that front room?"

"Wow!" Sara said later. "This isn't just food. It's a feast!"

I agreed. There were platters of chicken, casseroles, and even loaves of homemade bread! I kept my eye on a steaming crock of dark brown baked beans!

Sara and I helped arrange the desserts on our dining room table. We tried to decide which one looked best. But it was impossible to choose among apple pie, a pink cake, brownies with chocolate frosting, and a watermelon filled with fruit!

With the tables crosswise, there was room for everybody to eat in our front living room. Well, it was crowded, but that just made it more fun. Sara sat next to me, but the adults did most of the talking.

"You gals have outdone yourselves!" said a giant of a man.

"Don't forget there's supposed to be some food left for the Hoopers!" a woman teased.

"Did we tell you *we're* moving next month?" a man joked.

"Aha, but you aren't having a baby!" Mrs. Upjohn laughed.

After supper, everybody crowded into our family room to sing. Sara and I sat on the floor. So did lots of other people. In my entire life, I've never heard singing like that!

"I didn't know there were this many Christians in the entire world!" I told Sara. "In our last church, Jason and I were the only kids!"

At the end, everybody sang "How Great Thou Art" twice. That's when I first noticed that Sara didn't know the words.

And then everybody started going home.

"See you tomorrow!" someone said.

"I'll take Allison home! It's right on the way!"

"Somebody left a pie plate!"

"I'd better split, too," Sara said. "My mother will be getting home from work soon."

19

"Thanks for coming," I told her.

At last, the only people still here were Mr. and Mrs. Upjohn.

Dad just shook his head. "Our other church only had eleven people in it," he said. "And everybody lived about a hundred miles apart."

"You must have felt like pioneers up there all by yourselves!" Mrs. Upjohn said.

She's right! That's exactly how we did feel! But now the memory of all those friendly people buzzing around still seemed to fill Home Sweet Home.

"I'd like to invite you to visit our church tomorrow," Mr. Upjohn said. "In the summer, we meet at ten o'clock. Sunday school is afterwards."

"We'll be there," Dad told him.

"Unless, of course, we have to go to the hospital!" Mom said.

"If you need us for anything, just call," Mrs. Upjohn said. "We're only ten minutes away."

"How can we ever thank you!" Mom said. She was smiling, but I noticed she had tears in her eyes.

When they were gone, my family just stood in the kitchen and looked at each other.

"They left enough food to last us a week!" Mom said.

"And we won't have to go back to clean up the

cabin," Dad told her. "Two couples asked me for the key and said they'll take care of it!"

"It's wonderful how good God is!" Mom said.

We all agreed.

"You know what?" Jason said. "I think the Lord worked it all out even better than we could have done it ourselves!"

Lots of Changes

When we got home from Sunday school, Dad and Jason went on inside to set the table for lunch. I waited and walked with Mom. She kind of waddles along—like a duck.

Sara was waiting on our back steps. "Hi!" she said. "I was beginning to think you had gone to the hospital."

"We're still here, Sara," Mom said.

"So I see," Sara said. "Mrs. Hooper, are you sure there's a baby in there?"

Mom laughed. "I'm sure," she said. "I can feel the baby moving right now."

Sara's eyes got real big. "No kidding!"

"Sometimes he even kicks!" I said.

"No kidding!"

Mom eased herself down next to Sara. "Would you like to feel the baby move?"

"Oh, Mrs. Hooper, I couldn't do that!" Sara said. "Are you sure it's OK?"

"Go ahead," I said. "It's neat!"

Slowly Sara reached over. But her hand stopped about an inch from Mom's stomach.

"Don't be afraid, Sara," Mom said. She took Sara's hand and placed it on her abdomen.

"I don't feel a thing!" Sara said. "I mean, there has to be something in there all right. But it just feels like a watermelon!"

Both Mom and I laughed. "Just wait," I said.

All of a sudden, Sara's eyes got even bigger. "I can feel the baby moving!" she said. "Katie, put your hand next to mine!"

I reached down, and together we felt the baby move . . . and move . . . and move!

Mom laughed. "I think the newest Hooper is going to be a gymnast!"

"Really?" I asked. "Are you sure?" I could just picture a cute little kid doing flips!

"I'm just kidding," Mom admitted. "But I think this child is a lot more active than you and Jason were! Of course, maybe I just don't remember. It's been a long time since you were a baby!"

Just then Dad stuck his head out the door. "Time for lunch," he said. "Well, well! What's going on here?"

"Sara has never felt a baby move," Mom said. She reached back for balance and struggled to her feet. "We'll be right in, Steve."

"It was all over anyhow," Sara said. She stood up, too.

"Maybe you can come back later, after we eat," I said.

"What time?" Sara asked.

Mom turned around. "Have you forgotten, Katie? It's Family Day."

I had forgotten! "I'm sorry, but I can't play today," I told Sara. "It's Family Day."

"What's that?" she asked.

"It's when we Hoopers do special stuff together," I explained. "Doesn't your family ever do that?"

"Are you kidding!" Sara laughed, but her laugh had no joy in it.

I didn't know what to say. "So, Sara, how about it if we plan to get together tomorrow morning?"

"What time?" Sara asked.

I thought fast. "Why don't you come over about ten o'clock," I said.

"That's when "Gilligan's Island" is on," Sara said.

I felt impatient. "Well, it's up to you! If you'd rather sit around and watch soaps, then do it!"

"Maybe I will," Sara said. "See ya around!"

Halfway across our yard she turned and yelled, "And, by the way, Stupid, "Gilligan's Island" isn't a soap!"

I watched her go. Being Sara's friend isn't always easy. Then I turned and went inside.

At lunch, I glanced around the kitchen. Large boxes, still unopened, sat in the corner. "I was just thinking," I said, "it's going to seem funny having Family Day here in this house! Who's in charge today?" I knew it wasn't my turn. I did it last week.

"Yo!" Dad grinned from ear to ear. "You're looking at him. In person!"

"I'll bet it's a treasure hunt!" Jason guessed. "You have that *look* on your face!"

Dad kept grinning. "Maybe it is, and maybe it isn't!"

"I'll need to rest after lunch," Mom said. "I'm really tired."

"Some quiet time won't hurt any of us," Dad said.

Because we still had some paper plates left from last night, there were hardly any dishes. I spooned out one last taste of baked beans before I put the food back in the refrigerator.

"How was Sunday school?" Jason asked.

"Incredible!" I reported. "My teacher is beautiful, and the girls are nice, and I even knew the answer to a question!"

I waited for Jason to take a turn, but he didn't say anything. "Well?" I asked.

"It was OK," he said slowly. "Well, I guess I expected too much. After last night, I thought the guys would be friendlier. But all they talked about was their party. To be honest, I felt left out."

"Wait till next week," I said. "You'll make friends. I know you will."

I followed my brother upstairs. Mom and Dad's door was already closed. "See you later," Jason said. He closed his door behind him.

Nothing about my room seemed familiar. With my door closed, it was like being trapped in an ugly box! Sara was right. The walls are yucky! And, when I looked out the window, I couldn't see the mountains.

"What's happening to me?" I thought. "If God is making everything so wonderful, how come I feel this way?"

I pulled the blankets onto my bed. Ignoring the lumps, I sat down and closed my eyes.

"Lord, are you here or not?" I said out loud.

Actually, I already knew the answer. I know Jesus is always with me.

"It's so different," I told Him. "My whole world is changing. Family Day never meant I couldn't play with a friend. Not when I didn't even *have* friends!"

I sat quietly and waited.

"And what kind of a friend is Sara, anyhow?" I prayed. "Just because I don't know about her dumb TV program doesn't mean I'm stupid!"

Again I waited.

"I wonder what her family's like?"

That's when I started thinking about Jason. "He could use a friend, You know! He's never really had one. Well, there was Robert, but he's in Denver. Lord, could You give both Jason and Robert new friends? Please!"

I remembered last night. "Lord, thanks for sending the nice people to help us! And thanks for giving us this big house! And thanks that I have my own room!"

I could feel myself start to smile. I just couldn't help it!

"Heavenly Father, thank You for the new baby You're giving us! Please make it so that the baby is healthy! And don't forget to keep Mom safe! We need her a lot!" I waited. "Do You think it could be a girl?" Again I waited. "But actually, a cute little boy would be OK, too," I prayed.

"Lord, You know what! With my eyes closed, praying is the same as it was in my old room! Is that why You made our eyes so they can close? Thanks! And don't forget, I love You! Amen."

When I opened my eyes, my room looked the same. But I felt different.

Suddenly, I remembered my dolls! I had packed them in a box. There were only two big cartons in my room. When I pulled open the top of the first one, there they were!

As I lifted her from the box, Audrey smiled her weak little smile. "I thought you'd never get me out of there!" she said.

"Patience, patience!" I told her. I sounded just like my mother!

"This is a nice room," she said.

"It's going to be all right," I agreed. "Where would you like to sit—on the window sill again?"

"Ask Bronco Bob," the doll said.

"Well, how about it, B. B.?" I set Audrey on the bed and lifted him out of the carton.

"Whatever," he said. Although he's a souvenir from a Denver Broncos game, sometimes he sounds a lot like my father.

"Come on, Gomer! We need you, too!" I reached in and pulled out the floppy white lamb and gave him a hug.

Then Dad was knocking on my door. "Come on, Katie! Time for Family Day! Put on your oldest clothes and meet in the family room!"

"Coming, Dad," I yelled. "As soon as I get my own family settled!"

Grinning, I lined up the three dolls on the window sill. And suddenly my room felt like home!

A Place
for Our Baby

Dad, wearing paint-spattered jeans and shirt, stood smiling in the middle of the family room. Mom and Jason were already sitting on the couch.

"Today, we're going to spend our Family Day getting ready for the arrival of Baby Hooper!" Dad told us.

Mom laughed. "I'm already ready," she said.

"Aha, but the baby's room isn't ready! And *we* aren't ready!" Dad said.

Dad kept smiling. "You've probably already figured out that we're going to paint the nursery," he said. "But before we go upstairs, I want to tell you a little about what's been happening to our baby so far."

"I know," I said. "He's been growing!"

"Right," Dad smiled. "But not just growing larger. Baby Hooper has also been growing more complicated!" He picked up a book and showed us a picture of a baby still in his mother's womb.

"As you know, babies start out when a sperm cell from the father merges with an egg cell within the mother. Well, for about nine months now, those two cells have been multiplying two hundred billion times!"

I couldn't even imagine that number!

Almost as if he read my mind, Dad continued. "This book says that if a man had the skill to create a baby and could make one cell per minute, it would take him five hundred thousand years of continuous work."

Dad looked up. "And even if you had all the time in the world, could you do it?" Dad asked.

"Do what?" I asked. "Create a baby?"

Well, naturally we couldn't!

"Well, that's what God has done in about 265 days!" Dad said.

"I guess that's one reason birth is considered such a miracle!" Mom said.

"I thought that would be something neat to remember today," Dad said. Then he glanced at his watch and gave us each a new painting cap. Almost automatically, without a word, we all put them on.

31

We looked real dumb. When I looked around at my family, I started to giggle. Well, that got Mom started laughing, and we laughed until I felt weak.

"If we don't get started painting, we'll never finish!" Jason reminded us. It figured.

It didn't take long to clear out the baby's room. The crib rolled easily on little wheels. While I removed the boxes of diapers and stuff, my brother carried out the rocking chair. And then Dad helped Jason with the chest of drawers.

"Here, Elizabeth," Dad said. "You sit by the door in the rocking chair. You can be the chief inspector!"

Mom saluted. "Yes, Sir!" she said. "Assignment accepted, Sir!" Dad had to smile.

Then he handed Jason and me paintbrushes. "You two will be in charge of painting around the edges of the windows and doors!" Dad raised his hand in a salute.

Giggling, we saluted back.

"Yes, Sir!" Jason said. "I'll take the higher parts, Sir!"

"Assignment accepted, Sir!" I said.

Mom sat in the rocking chair looking at Dad's book. Meanwhile, Dad opened the paint can, stirred, and poured some paint into his roller pan.

"How come we're painting it white?" I asked.

"What's wrong with pink?"

Mom laughed. "I think you know, Katie."

To be honest, the walls in the nursery were just about as yucky as the ones in my room! I'm glad our baby won't have to open his eyes to see something so gross!

While I outlined one of the windows, I thought about what Dad had said earlier. "In the beginning, does a baby look like a baby?" I asked. "I mean when he just starts out?"

"It only takes a few weeks until he does," Dad said. "Your mother can show you the pictures in the book."

I stopped painting and looked at the drawings. I noticed that for the first few months, the baby's head was almost as big as the body! "But look at the tiny toes and fingers!" I said.

"The baby's heart starts to beat in the fourth week," Mom said. "And the doctor can hear his heartbeat after about twenty weeks."

Jason came to look, too. "But he looks just like a baby long before nine months!" he noticed. "Why can't he be born sooner?"

"Sometimes babies do come earlier," Mom explained. "Have you heard the expression *premature?* That describes a baby that is born sooner than nine months. Babies like that are small and sometimes have a very hard time staying alive."

"You mean they die?" I asked.

"Nowadays, doctors can do wonderful things to help premature babies make it!" Mom said. "But a tiny baby has to remain in the hospital until he is strong enough to go home."

"Hey," Dad said, "I've caught up with you! How about painting some more edges?"

"The room's starting to look wonderful!" Mom told us.

For a while, we were working so hard that nobody said anything. But at last we could relax.

"Can I try the roller?" Jason asked.

"Sure, but first watch how I do it," Dad said.

Afterwards, I even got a turn! But the part I painted looked all full of streaks!

"It's a good try, Katie!" Dad said. But I think everybody was glad when I decided to stick with my paintbrush!

When we were just about done, Dad started getting silly. He painted Mom's nose! And when we laughed at her, he painted Jason's and mine!

"Your turn!" Jason threatened.

"Oh, no you don't!" Dad laughed.

"Oh, yes we do!" I said.

"I'll hold him," Jason said. "Get your paintbrush, Katie!"

"Watch out or you'll step in the paint!" Mom yelled.

While everyone shrieked, I painted Dad's nose. And then, for good measure, I dabbed paint on both his cheeks.

Mom laughed. "The baby's father is a clown!"

Dad opened his eyes wide and pranced around the room. For such a large man, he is really very graceful!

"Let's finish up!" Mom said. "I'm hungry!"

"That's right," Jason said. "We have to make sure our baby gets enough to eat!"

"Does he like popcorn?" I asked.

Everybody laughed. Popcorn is our favorite Family Day snack.

"Before we take a break, we have to clean the roller and brushes," Dad said.

"And wash off our noses," I laughed.

"Let's leave them white for now," Mom said. "It would be lots of fun."

But we washed our noses after all. Dad said it might be harder to get the paint off later. "We can keep wearing our paint hats," he said. And, frankly, even that was pretty funny.

While we were eating our popcorn, Jason was real quiet. "Is something wrong, Son?" Dad asked.

My brother grinned. "I was just thinking about the baby eating popcorn," he said. "I guess I don't know what really happens."

"I can tell you," Mom said. "A baby gets his

35

food and oxygen through the umbilical cord. Everybody has one! Did you know that your navel, or bellybutton, is where your umbilical cord was fastened on before you were born?"

"Mom, how do you feed the baby?" I asked.

"You mean now, before birth?" Mom asked.

I nodded.

"I haven't even had to think about it!" Mom said. "Of course, you know I eat healthy foods. But the Lord has worked out a system of feeding the baby through something called a *placenta.* It's just about as automatic as our breathing or digesting food!"

"So, no popcorn!" Jason smiled.

"Not today, anyway," Mom said. "But just wait! Every Hooper likes popcorn. You'll see!"

"OK, gang," Dad said, "let's go up and put the nursery back in order!"

Putting everything back into a newly-painted room is always lots of fun! And this time, because of the baby, it was even more special.

"I can just picture him lying in the crib!" I said. "He's kicking his little legs!"

"But can you hear him crying?" Dad teased.

Mom laughed. "I can," she said.

"Where shall we put the chest of drawers?" Jason asked.

"Let's try it over here," Mom said. "That's where we'll be changing the baby's diapers."

"Count me out!" Jason said.

"Count him in!" Dad laughed. "Jason, if I can do it, you can!"

"Doesn't the nursery look wonderful!" Mom said. "And when I have time, I'll make curtains."

I patted Mom's stomach. "We're all set! Your next place is ready for you, little baby!"

And just then he moved! "See," I said, "I think he heard me!"

Everybody laughed.

Another "Ghost"

After we ate, I was helping in the kitchen.
"Katie, have you fed the dog?" Dad asked.

I stood there and just looked at him.

"You'd better do it now," he said. "Once we start reading, you won't want to interrupt the story."

Suddenly, I could hardly breathe. To be honest, I hadn't even thought about January since we got to Woodland Park. What was even worse, I couldn't even remember *seeing* him!

I was overwhelmed with guilt feelings. I remembered how I had begged to keep the darling puppy. And I can still hear my parents' voices saying I was too irresponsible!

"I'll be there in a few minutes," I said.

"Don't be long," Dad said. "If we start now, maybe we can even read several chapters." He left to join Mom and Jason in the family room.

Since everybody could see that the dog wasn't in the kitchen, I headed for the dining room. I looked behind the boxes of dishes. I even looked inside the fireplace. But January wasn't there either.

My heart was pounding. I wanted to call January's name, but I couldn't. I didn't want my family to know my awful secret!

"Katie, we're waiting for you!" Jason called.

I walked across the front hall and stuck my head into the family room. "Go ahead and start without me," I said. "I have to go upstairs for a minute."

"Katie, are you sick?" Mom asked. "You look like you don't feel well."

I tried to smile. "I'll be all right," I said. "I just need to go to my room." I grabbed the banister and took the stairs two at a time.

A quick look into my room proved what I suspected. Although Audrey, B. B., and Gomer were there, my dog was not.

Jason's door was closed. Gently I turned the knob. The door squeaked as I slowly pushed it open. I couldn't believe it! We're here one day and my brother's room is neat already! Everything was put away, and his bedspread was as tight as a drum! No one ever thinks *he* is irresponsible!

I gave a puny whistle. To be honest, I didn't really figure January would be hiding under Jason's bed. And he wasn't.

Looking for the dog in the nursery seemed downright silly. We had been painting in there all afternoon. Still, I stuck my head in. Spotting the closet, I checked that out, too. You guessed it! No dog!

I discovered that my parents' room is a mess. Stuff all over the bed! Boxes piled against the wall! I quietly picked my way across the room. Because now I was right above where my family was waiting!

My parents' bedroom is the one with a secret passageway in the closet. But I couldn't really go in there without a flashlight. So I stuck my head in and whispered. "January! January! January!"

"Katie, what are you doing up there?" My father's voice was strong and firm.

"Nothing," I said.

"Nonsense," Dad said. "Come down here right now, and tell me what you're doing in our bedroom."

When I walked into the family room, everybody was looking right at me.

"OK, Katie, tell me about it," Dad said.

I looked down at the floor. "I was looking for something."

"Would you like to tell us what?" Dad said.

"Not really," I said. "I mean, I wish I didn't have to tell you."

"You might as well get it over with," Jason said.

"I don't know how to say this," I said. "I think I lost my dog."

"January's gone?" Mom asked. "Come to think of it, I haven't seen him all day."

"When was the last time you saw him?" Dad asked.

I tried to think. "I guess I don't remember seeing him at the party. Do you?"

"You didn't feed him last night?" Jason said.

I felt miserable. "I forgot," I said. "Sara came up to my room with me. And there were so many people around. And then we helped set the table. And then we sang. And ... everything."

"Oh, my," Mom said. "Did anyone bring January into the house?"

Everybody just looked at each other.

"I was helping unload the truck," Dad said.

"I was telling people where to put things," Mom said.

"He isn't my dog," Jason said.

"Don't tell me we left January at the cabin!" Dad said.

"No," I remembered. "He was riding with Jason and me in Purple Jeep. I remember he woke up and snorted."

"So at least we know he's here in Woodland Park," Mom said.

"At least he was yesterday," Jason said.

Nobody said a word about my lack of responsibility. I was thankful. Although, frankly, if they had, I don't think I could have felt much worse!

"We'd better go out and look for him," Dad said. "He's never been a dog to wander far. He could even be in the yard."

We put on sweaters and went out through the kitchen door. Well, Dad, Jason, and I went out. Mom stayed inside. Dad said he didn't want her to get all tired out.

From the back porch, Dad called, "January!" But nothing happened. "I think we'd better split up," he said. "But don't go far! It will be dark before we know it."

As I headed off alone, I remembered to pray. "Please, Lord, help us!" Then I walked toward Sara's house.

"January! January!" I called.

As I passed the house next to ours, a door opened, and a man stuck his head out.

"January!" I called.

"No!" the man called back. "It's August!" He laughed.

42

"Have you seen my dog?" I asked.

"No, I haven't," he said.

I've never been inside Sara's house. I walked past slowly, but I didn't see any signs of life. "January! Where are you, January?"

I walked just a little farther. In the background, I could faintly hear Jason calling. "January! January!" Finally, I turned around and started back.

As I neared Home Sweet Home, I glanced up at the turret. There wouldn't be a ghost there now! But I couldn't believe my eyes!

There, in the window of the third floor tower, was January!

I started to run. "Dad! Jason!" I called. "I found him!"

My brother was the first to reach me. "Where is he?" he asked.

I pointed. "Look!" I laughed. "Up in the tower! We have another ghost!"

Jason laughed, too. "How do you suppose he got up there?"

"I don't know. I guess the door must have been open," I said.

My father seldom runs, and this time was no exception. As he approached, I pointed to the tower. Dad's face broke into a huge smile. "Well, well," he said. "Another ghost!"

"I'll go and get him," I said. "He must be real

hungry and thirsty!"

"Wonderful!" Mom said, when we told her. "I'm so glad you found him!"

As soon as I opened the door to the third floor stairway, January jumped out! He ran past me and skidded on the hall floor. Then he turned and looked at me.

"January!" I said. "Come here. I'm sorry!"

Slowly, he came and stood in front of me. Then, as I rubbed his head, he wagged his tail.

"Let's go down!" I told him. "I won't ever forget about you again, January! I promise!"

Well, I've never seen a dog drink his water so fast! Or gulp down his food like that!

Later, back in the family room, January sat right at my feet while Dad read our story. We only got to read one chapter, but nobody blamed me.

And by the time I went to bed, I'd even stopped blaming myself!

Sara's Secret

After breakfast, Dad and Jason went to the hardware store, and I helped Mom put baby clothes away in the chest of drawers.

"Was I really this size?" I asked. The undershirt looked like it would fit Audrey, my doll.

"You were small," Mom said. "You only weighed a little over six pounds. Six pounds, one ounce, to be exact! And Jason wasn't much bigger."

"Was it hard waiting for us to be born?"

"Jason surprised everybody and came early," Mom said. "Doctors can only estimate a birth date. Babies come when they're ready!"

"How about me? Were you surprised when I was born on Valentine's day?"

Mom laughed. "The doctor figured you'd be born on February 12, Lincoln's birthday! That's why before you were born we nicknamed you Abraham!"

"Abraham! You're kidding!" I said.

"No, I'm not. I can remember feeling almost afraid to pray for a girl! But I guess the Lord knew how much I wanted one!" Mom said.

"How about this baby?" I asked. "Now you already have a boy and a girl."

"I'm praying for a healthy child," Mom said.

I grinned. "Maybe we'll get twins!"

"No, it isn't twins," Mom said. "There's only one heartbeat."

"Do you have a name all picked out?" I asked.

She smiled. "We do. Actually, two names—one for a boy and one for a girl."

"So?" I waited.

"Wouldn't you rather be surprised?"

"Please tell me now!" I begged.

But she didn't. What Mom did do was teach me how to fold diapers! I wasn't too good at getting the extra layers folded in the middle, but Mom was patient. She said I'll be getting lots of practice!

At ten o'clock I started watching for Sara. "She might be late," I said. "She could be watching television." But she didn't come at half past ten either.

"Why don't you go over to her house?" Mom said. "You don't always have to wait for Sara to come here."

"Good idea!" I said. "I think I'll take January with me."

As we walked along, I realized I had never been able to just walk over to someone's house. At the cabin, we didn't have any close neighbors. The truth is, Sara is my first real friend.

"It's no big deal!" I told January. "We're just going to ring the doorbell, that's all."

I did it. Nothing happened.

"They probably didn't hear me," I said. I tried again. Still nothing happened.

"She's probably not home," I said. "Come on, January. Let's go!"

We had just turned away when the door opened. It was Sara, all right. Her red hair stuck out in every direction. But today she wasn't smiling. "I thought I saw you through the window," she said. "I didn't think you liked me."

"Of course, I like you!" I said. "I just couldn't play yesterday. On Sundays we have Family Day."

"Every week?" she asked.

I nodded. "We've done it all my life."

"I never heard of Family Day before," Sara said.

"Well, you have now," I said. Then we just stood and looked at each other.

"I guess I'm kind of uptight," she said. "I'm really not supposed to answer the door when Mom's gone."

"Where does your mother work?" I asked.

"Downtown. She's a waitress."

"Oh," I said.

"I'm not supposed to let anyone in either," Sara said. Then she smiled. "But I guess it wouldn't hurt. After all, Katie, you're my best friend. Want to see my room?"

I grinned. "Sure."

"You'll have to leave January outside. Mom doesn't allow animals in here," she said.

My smile faded. "Then I can't stay long. I promised myself I'd take better care of him."

I followed Sara inside. Her house is small, smaller even than our cabin. My first look at the living room reminded me of Jason. Not a single thing was out of place! It looked kind of like a shoe box with two windows in it.

"It's nice," I said. "Nice and cozy."

"How about this for a television set!" she said.

"Nice," I said.

"What do you mean, *nice?* I mean, is that large screen, or what!" she said.

"It's large," I agreed. "The people must look as big as life."

"Bigger," Sara said.

Behind the living room was a little square kitchen. And everything in there was hidden away. I mean, there wasn't even a drinking glass next to the sink!

"Nice," I said. "I like the wallpaper."

"It was already here when we came," Sara said.

"I've always liked ducks," I said.

"My mother hates them," Sara said.

As we walked past, I couldn't help glancing into the front bedroom. It had white furniture and a pink bedspread. And no clutter!

Now Sara stood in the doorway of the last room. "Well, here it is!" she said. "What do you think?"

"I like it, Sara!" I said.

She grinned. "I thought you were going to say 'Nice!'"

I grinned back. "Which bed do you sleep in, the top or the bottom?" I couldn't tell just by looking at them.

"It depends," Sara said.

"I've never seen such a *neat* house," I told her. "Ours is a mess!"

"So I've noticed."

"Of course, Home Sweet Home is old. And naturally it takes a while to get settled after you move." My voice trailed off. The truth is that our cabin was always messy, too! And somehow I had the feeling Sara knew it!

"Mom says there are two kinds of people—those who save and those who don't," Sara said.

"Then I guess we're savers," I said. "Except for Jason."

All of a sudden Sara's voice got very soft. And her eyes got big. "Katie, do you want to see something?" she whispered.

"Sure!" I whispered back.

"Well, come on in!" She pulled her bedroom door closed behind us. Then she opened a dresser drawer and took out a small box. She carefully removed a flat package wrapped in tissue paper.

"What is it?" I asked. "Is it a treasure?"

"Not exactly," she said. "Well, sort of." She un-wrapped a small picture and handed it to me. "Well, what do you think?"

I looked at the smiling face. "Nice," I said. We both giggled when I said it. "Who is he?"

"He's my father. Mom would kill me if she knew I have this!" Sara's very dramatic. I think it's because she watches so much television.

"Why would she kill you?"

Sara's eyes got even bigger. "Because I think she hates him!"

"Why would your mother hate your father?"

"Because he disappeared," Sara whispered.

"Your father left you? Why did he do that?"

Sara shrugged her shoulders. "Mom never told me. And I'm afraid to ask."

"When did he go away?" I asked.

"When I was a baby," Sara said.

"Sara, you mean you never knew your father?" I couldn't believe it.

"That's right," Sara said. "Katie, you're the very first person I ever told. And now you've got to promise you'll never tell another soul!"

Lost Again!

I looked at the picture one more time and handed it back to Sara. "I won't tell anyone about your father," I promised. "Where did you get the picture?"

"From my grandmother," Sara said.

"Where does your grandmother live?"

Sara looked down at the floor. "She used to live in Omaha," she said. "But she died."

Suddenly, I wanted to hug Sara like I hug Audrey. But I didn't. "Is that where you used to live? In Omaha?"

Sara nodded. Her eyes weren't big now. They were full of tears. "Mom said there was no using hanging around there any longer. So we moved out here last month."

"I'm glad you came to Colorado," I said. "You'll like it here."

"We're going to learn to ski," she said. "Katie, can you ski?"

"Not downhill. Actually, I don't have skis."

"Me either. I'm saving up though." Now her eyes were big again. When they get like that, I think she looks kind of like a clown. But I've never told her that. What's the point?

Suddenly, I remembered my dog. "I'd better check on January. Did I tell you he got lost last night?"

"Just a second. I'll go with you." Sara wrapped up her father's picture again and carefully returned it to its hiding place.

"Don't forget, Katie! You promised you'd never tell," she said. "Even if they pull out your fingernails! Right?"

"Right," I said. Although now I felt less sure about it.

"Someday he's coming back!" Sara said. Her eyes got even bigger. "Someday my father's coming back to rescue me!"

I'm not sure what she meant. I do know that sharing her secret somehow makes me feel different about her.

As we were leaving Sara's room, she smiled. "It's neat to have a friend."

I smiled, too. "It's funny. I was just thinking

exactly the same thing! Sara, did you really ask Jesus to send you a friend, too?"

"I never said I did that!"

"I thought you did," I said. "Remember the first time we met? I was baby-sitting January in Purple Jeep. I thought you told me you had prayed for a friend."

"Sure," Sara said. "I said that."

"Then why did you say you didn't?"

"I said I prayed," Sara said. "But I never said I asked anybody about it!"

As I stepped outside, I looked around for my dog. "Oh, no!"

"What's wrong?" Sara asked.

I looked up and down the sidewalk. "I can't believe it! January's gone again!"

"You weren't inside more than ten minutes," she said.

"I know. But I don't see him anywhere!" I walked to the corner of the house and looked back. Then I started to call. "January! January! Jan ... u ... ary!"

"He couldn't have gone far," Sara said. "Didn't you tell him to wait right here! I'm sure you only left him for a few minutes."

"I'll have to hunt for him," I said. "Want to come with me?"

"I have to leave a note," she said.

While I waited, I tried to figure out where

January could be. Sometimes the stupid dog just falls asleep somewhere. But around Sara's yard there aren't a lot of places to nap.

"OK, I'm ready," Sara said. She locked the front door and put the key into her jeans. "I doubt if you were in my house more than thirty seconds!"

"I feel rotten," I said. "I guess it's true. I'm not very responsible."

"It wasn't your fault," Sara said. "Is it your fault if the dumb dog doesn't obey?"

"I never had this problem when we lived in the cabin," I said. "Well, hardly ever."

"Where did you find him last night?" Sara asked.

I grinned. "You'll never guess! Tell me, what do you think of when I say *ghost!*" I laughed.

"You mean he was in the tower?" She giggled. "Maybe he's up there now!"

"We could check it out," I said. "Let's go!"

We ran all the way. But when we stopped in front of my house to look up at the turret, January wasn't in the window.

"What if he wasn't alone last night!" Sara said. "Maybe January was hiding up there with another ghost!"

Well, to make a long story short, he wasn't! Sara was too afraid to go up into the turret, so I had to check it out by myself.

"The tower's empty," I reported. "Have you got any other ideas?"

"It's your dog!" Sara said. "How come I have to do all the thinking!"

"I just remembered. I can ask Jesus," I told her.

"Who's Jesus?" Sara asked.

I just looked at her. "You're faking," I said. "You must know who Jesus is!"

"I've heard of it," Sara said. "Mom's friend says it all the time."

"She swears?" I asked.

"Sure. All the time."

"Sara, don't you know Jesus is a real person?"

"No kidding!" she said. "Where does He live?"

"He lives everywhere," I explained. "But you can't see Him."

"What does that mean?" she asked.

"Sara, haven't you ever gone to Sunday school?"

"Nope."

I smiled. "Want to come with me next week?"

"I might. I'll think about it," she said.

"Wouldn't you like to learn about God?"

"Him I've heard of!" Sara said.

"Well, Jesus is God's Son!" I told her.

"No kidding!" she said. "I didn't know He had any kids!"

"Sara, I think you'd better come with me next Sunday!"

"I told you I'd think about it," she said. "Actually, that's the only morning all week that my mother doesn't go to work."

"Oh," I said.

Just then Mom came into the kitchen. "Hi, girls!" she said. "I thought I heard voices."

"Mrs. Hooper, your dog's lost," Sara said. "But don't blame Katie. She only came into my house for half a second!"

"Oh, my!" Mom said. "I think maybe we should pray about it."

"That's just what I was telling her," I said. "Mom, will you do it?"

"Of course," Mom said. She closed her eyes. "Lord, we've misplaced our dog again! Please show us where he is! And please help January not to be frightened. In Jesus' name, Amen."

"Wow!" Sara said. "Is this kind of like God's lost and found or something?"

Mom laughed. "Kind of," she said. "Mostly Jesus finds lost people!"

Mary had a little lamb! It was Purple Jeep's horn. "Dad's home!" I said.

"Look who we found!" Jason said. "January was sitting by the side of the road!"

I ran over and hugged my dog.

"I think January was hitchhiking!" Dad laughed. "He had one paw in the air!"

"I can't believe it!" Sara said.

58

"January's always doing something funny!" I said. "Did you see his picture in the newspaper—the time he ate an ice cream cone?"

Sara shook her head. "Wow!" she said. "I think I'll notify the networks. What goes on at your house is a lot better than most of the stuff you see on TV!"

We Search for Fame

After lunch, Sara and I sat down on the back stairs. I was determined not to let January out of my sight. As we talked, I rubbed his fur. And, naturally, he fell asleep.

"Katie, I'm glad I told you about my father," Sara said.

"Do you really think he'll try to find you?"

"Don't talk so loud," she said.

"I'm sorry."

Sara's eyes got big. "He's going to rescue me!" she said. "You've heard about handsome princes who rescue damsels in distress! Well, my prince happens to have a face just like my father!"

"But that's just in storybooks," I said. "Sara, pardon me, but you aren't Cinderella! You can't really still believe in fairy tales!"

"Why not?" she asked. "A person has to believe in something! And when it comes to happy endings, you can always count on a prince!"

"You're putting me on!" I said.

"Well, I know my father isn't really a prince." Sara grinned. "I'm not as dumb as I look!"

"Right," I said.

"But I've seen enough television to know my father's trying to find me!" Sara paused. "The trouble is I'm not sure he knows where to look!"

"Do you think he knows you've moved to Colorado?" I asked.

"That's a problem!" Sara said. "Even if he thinks of Colorado, he'll probably be checking out Denver or a ski resort. He'll never think of looking for me in a two-bit town like Woodland Park!"

"You're probably right," I said.

"You're no help!" Sara said. "I hate it when you always agree with me!"

"Well, do you expect me to act like we live in the center of the universe?"

"There has to be some way to let him know I'm here," Sara said.

"It's too bad you aren't famous," I said. "Then the whole world would know you're here!"

"You know, that's a good idea!" Sara said.

"It is?"

"Sure. That's it! All I have to do is get famous!" She laughed.

"What are you good at?" I asked. "Can you sing?"

She laughed again. "I nearly ruined our fourth-grade chorus! I'm so bad my teacher made me be a mouth-mover!"

"Well, forget singing! My brother taught himself to play the guitar."

"So what? He's not famous! Has anybody ever heard of Jason Hooper?"

"Maybe you could win a beauty contest or something," I said.

"That's an idea!" She looked thoughtful.

I didn't have the heart to tell her I was just kidding. "Or maybe you could win a spelling bee," I said.

"No way!" Sara said. "Besides, the school year hasn't even started yet."

We were just sitting there thinking. Suddenly, January woke up, snorted, and rolled over. All four of his legs were waving in the air! We laughed our heads off. After a few minutes, the dog rolled over again and went back to sleep.

"Did I hear you say January got his picture in the newspaper?" Sara asked.

"He was on the front page of the *Ute Pass Courier!*" I said proudly. "He was eating an ice cream cone."

"When was that?"

"A few weeks ago," I said.

"That's it!" Sara said. "I just have to think up a way to get my picture in the paper! Then my father will see it and rescue me!"

"It might work," I said. "We have a couple of days to think of something. The paper doesn't come out again until Thursday."

"Hi, Sara," Jason said. "Seen any ghosts lately?"

"Do you have to keep bringing that up?" she said. "Where'd you get the boxes?"

"From moving," he said. "We have a million of them." Jason dumped some cartons on top of an already huge pile and then disappeared around the side of the house.

"I've got it!" Sara said. "We can build a tower out of boxes! And when we get it tall enough, I can sit up on top. I could even be holding an American flag!"

"Why? I don't get it," I said.

She just looked at me. "Don't you understand about publicity? If you want your picture in the newspaper, you have to do something special! Something nobody else is doing!"

I remembered January and his ice cream cone. "Maybe you're right!" I said. "Maybe they'll think you're the Statue of Liberty!"

Sara thought a minute. "Maybe what I hold

should have a little more to do with Colorado. I could hold up a ski!"

"Or a mountain!" I said. But she didn't hear me.

Sara was already sorting through the discarded boxes in back of our house. "Take the biggest ones first," she said. "We need to build a strong base at the bottom."

Finding boxes the same size wasn't easy. But we finally assembled enough to form the foundation of the tower.

"Now we need the next size smaller," she said. "You get the idea!"

I got the idea, all right. But I was sure it would never work. No way were we going to build a tower strong enough for Sara to sit on. With or without an American flag!

"The boxes won't hold you," I said. "They aren't sturdy enough."

"Trust me," she said. "Just sort out the boxes and trust me."

The lower layers weren't all that difficult. We could stand around the base and stack boxes on. But it didn't take long until we were having trouble adding more to the top.

"Maybe your brother could help us," Sara said.

"He'd never go for this," I said. "Never in a million years! He'd draw up plans and build it out of lumber. And it would take him weeks."

"We don't have to tell him what the tower's for!" Sara said.

Actually, Jason was glad to stack up another layer of boxes for us. I happen to think he must be pretty desperate for a friend of his own!

"How's that, girls?" he asked. "Anything else you need?"

"As a matter of fact, yes," Sara said. "I could use a ladder! And I need something to represent sports in the state of Colorado."

"Dad just finished with the ladder," Jason said. "Hang on! I'll be right back!"

Pretty soon he was back dragging the ladder and carrying a football pennant he'd taken down off of his bedroom wall.

Later, after my brother left again, Sara looked thoughtful. "Actually, this is even better!" she said. "I really like the idea of the Denver Bronco pennant! It's pretty dumb to wave a ski around at the beginning of football season!"

"Come on. I'll hold the ladder," I said.

"Not yet!" Sara said. "There's nobody here to take my picture!"

"Sara, maybe you should just try it out first," I said.

"Good thinking!" she said. "And when they take the picture, I'm going to be wearing a dress! The first time my father sees me, I don't want to look like this!"

I held the ladder. Sara climbed slowly, the Bronco pennant clutched in her left hand. "Be careful!" I said.

I watched while she eased her left foot onto the tower of boxes. Incredibly, they held her.... At first!

"Watch out!" I yelled. "You're falling!"

Afterwards, I climbed on the pile of boxes with Sara, and we jumped around and laughed our heads off!

"To tell you the truth, I never did think it would work!" Sara gasped.

"Really?" I laughed.

"Really!"

At last, we collapsed on the ground, next to the remains of Sara's tower. We were weak from laughing. But every time, just when things got quiet, one of us would start laughing again!

"Getting your picture in the newspaper really isn't *that* bad of an idea!" I said.

"Publicity is a fabulous idea!" Sara said. "But I need another angle. Be honest, Katie. Do you really think I'd have a chance in a beauty contest?"

Sara Tries
Another Way

"I've got another idea!" Sara said. "If I can think up a way to make Woodland Park famous, they'll just have to put my picture in the paper!"

"Sara Wilcox, you're a genius!" I said.

She grinned and nodded.

"How do towns get famous?" I asked.

"I don't exactly know," she said. "I think it helps if a famous person was born there."

"Some are state capitals," I realized. "But I think Woodland Park is too late!"

"Well, they sure have great mountains here!" she said. "But I guess lots of towns in Colorado could be famous for that."

"They don't all have Pikes Peak!"

Sara rose to her feet. "That's it!" she said.

"Katie, just listen to this! What if I planned a gigantic birthday party for Pikes Peak! I could organize a parade that would put Woodland Park on the map!"

It was fun watching my friend get so excited! Her eyes sparkled! I smiled, enjoying her enthusiasm.

"We could sponsor a beauty contest to find a queen!" she said. "And how about a rodeo? I know there are enough horses here for a rodeo!"

Suddenly, I realized what she was saying. "Guess what?" I said. "You're too late!"

"What do you mean?"

"Woodland Park already has all that! Plus a street dance! And a pancake breakfast besides! They even have a car race up Pikes Peak!"

"You mean somebody took my idea?"

"Somebody else thought of it first," I told her. "It's called the Stampede Rodeo, and it happens early in July!"

"We moved here July 17. I must have just missed it," Sara said.

I felt rotten. "I'm not sure it's really a birthday party," I said. "But frankly, I think you'll have to come up with something else!"

Sara sat down. Her voice got soft and flat. "Katie, how can I ever get famous? How will my father find me?"

I looked at her. "Sara, are you sure you

couldn't just ask your mother about him?"

"If you knew my mother, you wouldn't say that!" she replied.

Frankly, I've always felt that Sara gets scared too easily. "What do you think she'd do to you?" I asked.

Sara rolled her eyes. "I hate to have to say it out loud!" she said.

"Tell me," I whispered.

Sara leaned down. She spoke slowly. "Katie, have you ever heard of the Chinese Death Torture?"

I shook my head.

"Well, my mother invented it!" she said, with pride in her voice.

I was kind of impressed. "Is your mother Chinese?" I asked.

"Don't be silly!" she said.

"Sara, I think you watch too much television!"

"Watch it!" Sara said. "I thought we were friends!"

"But sometimes friends disagree, don't they?"

"Not my friends," she said. "And not when it comes to TV."

It was pointless to continue the discussion. So I didn't say anything else. We sat in silence.

Finally, Sara spoke. "Did you go to the rodeo?"

"I did. It was wonderful!"

"How about the parade?"

"It was the best I've ever seen," I said. "Of course, I've never seen a parade anywhere else!"

"Well, you've never seen a good parade until you've seen one in Omaha!" Sara said.

"Maybe they'll let you be on the committee here," I said. "I bet you could give Woodland Park a few ideas!"

"The next parade is almost a year off!" she said. "Besides, it's not good enough just being on a committee. I need to be the chairperson! The big enchilada! The star!"

"Good luck!" I said.

"Of course, once I'm famous, they'll probably invite me to be the parade marshall," Sara said. She thought a minute. "You know what? I hate being nobody! It's depressing."

"I thought the whole point of getting famous was to locate your father!" I said. "Sara, why don't you just put an ad in the newspaper? You don't have to be famous to advertise!"

"No, but you need money!" she said.

"How much have you got?"

"About nine dollars," Sara said. "But I'm saving up for skis!"

"You probably could get a small ad for nine dollars," I said. I tried to think of what she could say. *"Beautiful Woodland Park redhead seeks to contact her father."*

"Thanks for trying, Katie," she said. "But I

really think I need a picture. Something my father can recognize. And big enough so my face shows. It can't be that hard to get famous!"

"Sara, there is another way," I said slowly.

"I hope it's something really original!" she said.

"Well," I grinned, "it's not exactly original. But it could work!"

"Try me!"

"We could ask Jesus to help you find your father!" I said.

Sara slapped her forehead with her hand. "An incredible idea!" she said. "Any why not? I forgot all about God's lost and found! But before we pray, will you just give me time to go home and change my clothes?"

"How come?"

"I don't want my father to find me dressed like this!" she said.

"Well, it might not happen immediately," I told her. "You have to realize that finding January just happened to be pretty easy."

"You mean God can't do it if it's hard?" she asked.

"I didn't say that! But something this hard might take Him a little longer!"

Sara didn't say anything. She just sat there and stared straight ahead. Finally, she spoke. "Katie, can you tell me how to pray? Or do we have to ask your mother?"

"I can help you," I said. "The Lord doesn't make kids wait until they grow up."

"On second thought, will you do the praying for me?" she asked.

I sat there and thought about it. "No, Sara," I said, finally. "It's your father. You'll have to do it yourself."

"But I don't have a script!" she said. "I could blow my lines!"

"There aren't any lines," I said. "Talking to Jesus is like talking to anybody else. You just make it up as you go along!"

"Improvise," Sara said. "When you don't have a script, it's called improvising."

"Whatever," I said. "The main thing is to just be respectful! After all, don't forget, you'll be talking to God Himself!"

"I know," she said. "He's the Star of the whole show! That's why I wanted a script!"

"Now, calm down, Sara. We're both going to close our eyes, and you're going to pray."

"Out loud?"

"Out loud! God wants to help you, but first you have to ask!" I closed my eyes and waited.

At first, nothing happened. "I feel stupid," Sara said, finally.

"Go on! I'm waiting!"

"Dear God," Sara prayed. "Please help me!

Can't You find me a father somewhere? I realize I'm not beautiful.... And I get scared all the time.... But it's so *awful* not to belong to anybody!"

As I listened, my eyes filled with tears.

And then I heard my friend sobbing. "It's no use, Katie," she said. "Somebody like God would never listen to somebody like me!"

I put my arms around her. "I love you, Sara," I told her. "And God loves you, too."

"It's no use," she said.

"It might take a little while for God to answer your prayer, but you'll see!" I told her. "And whether you know it or not, Sara, He does love you!"

A New Look at My Family

Even after Sara went home, I couldn't get her out of my mind! I think this is the first time I've really realized that not everybody has a wonderful family like mine!

At supper, I looked around at my parents and my brother. Before we sit down, we always stand in back of our chairs and sing. "Praise God, from whom all blessings flow . . ."

"How come the Lord gives our family so many blessings?" I asked, when we sat down.

"He loves us," Dad said.

"God is good," Mom said.

"He knows we love Him, and we're trying to serve Him," Jason added.

"But don't lots of people do that and still have

a rotten life?" I asked. "How about the poor people in Haiti?"

"Katie's right," Dad said. "Loving God and serving Him is no guarantee that we won't have troubles!"

"What we're talking about is called *grace*," Mom told us. "*Grace* means we receive blessings we don't deserve. God gives them anyway—because He's good and He loves us."

"I sure hope God loves Sara," I said. "I told her He does."

"You never have to worry about that, Katie," Dad said. "God loves *everybody!*"

"Including Sara?" I asked.

Dad smiled. "Including Sara!"

I felt better. It was hard not to tell everybody what Sara told me. But a promise is a promise!

After we finish eating, Dad always reads from his Bible. "Tonight our passage tells us about babies before they are born," he said.

"I've heard of babies," Mom said. Her eyes twinkled. "Aren't they those cute little dolls that grow up into teenagers?"

Dad smiled at her. "Please pay attention, Elizabeth!" he teased. "You just might learn something! This is from Psalm 139. I'll start reading beginning with verse 13:

"For you created my inmost being; you knit me

together in my mother's womb.

I praise you because I am fearfully and won-
derfully made; your works are wonderful, I
know that full well.

My frame was not hidden from you when I was
made in the secret place.

When I was woven together in the depths of the
earth, your eyes saw my unformed body.

All the days ordained for me were written in
your book before one of them came to be."

"Well, Katie, what do you think? Who's been taking care of our baby's development so far?" Dad asked.

"The Lord has," I said. "It sounds like He knows a lot more about our baby than we do! Does He really know whether the baby is a boy or a girl?"

"He knows even more than that," Mom said. "Every baby is one-of-a-kind!"

"But in the beginning aren't they all pretty much alike?" Jason asked.

"Not at all," Mom said. "God makes every baby different—special! And hidden inside his tiny body are lots of secret things that can never be changed! Things like the color of his eyes, how tall he'll grow, what he looks like, his personality, even certain talents."

"Could our baby have red hair?" I asked.

"I doubt it," Mom said. "What children look like is usually inherited from their parents. Or from their parents' families—like grandparents, or aunts and uncles. I don't think we have any red hair on either side of the family."

"So I'm tall because you are?" Jason asked.

"Probably," Dad said.

"Could our baby look like Jason? Or me?" I asked.

"Usually there's some family resemblance. But we'll have to wait and see!" Dad said.

"If he's bald, it's your fault!" I laughed.

"You said sometimes we inherit talents," Jason said. "Dad, you're an artist. How come neither Katie or I can draw?"

"I don't know," Dad said. "In fact, I have no idea where my own talent came from. I don't know of a single artist in my family. Sometimes God's gifts are total surprises!"

"It's another example of *grace,*" Mom said.

"Well, I don't care about our baby's talents!" I said. "I can't wait to hold him!"

Mom smiled. "Katie, you have the right idea! What every baby needs most is love!"

"But how will he know we love him?" I asked.

"You can tell him you do—all the time!" she said.

"But he won't be able to understand what we say, will he?" Jason asked.

"Babies understand," Mom said. "Long before they know what words mean, they can tell when people love them!"

"God has taken wonderful care of our baby so far," Dad said. "Can you think of anything we can do to make the Hooper home a good place for our baby to grow up?"

"We can help Mom so she won't have to do all the extra work alone and get tired and crabby," Jason said.

"What?" Mom laughed. "Me, crabby?"

"It's always a distinct possibility," Dad teased. "I can still remember when these two were babies!"

"Jason, when you were two, I was tempted to send you back where you came from!" Mom said.

"Can you do that?" I asked.

"Not really," Mom said. "He's still here, isn't he?"

Everybody laughed. "Let's change the subject!" Jason said. "I know something else we can do to help our baby have a good home. We can teach him about Jesus!"

Naturally, everybody agreed.

"There's one more thing," Mom said. "Let's always remember that every baby is special, one-of-a-kind! We want to encourage him to be whatever God has planned for him!"

"It sounds as if we're ready to welcome our

new little Hooper!" Dad said. "In our prayer time, let's pray again for his safe arrival."

At the end of every devotional time, we always pray out loud together. Suddenly, I think for the first time, I realized that all families don't do that!

"Thank You, Lord, for sending us another child!" Dad said. "Help us to make our home a wonderful place for him to grow up!"

"Thank You for the wonderful children we already have!" Mom said.

"Lord, please keep Mom safe! And, if it's Your will, give us a healthy baby!" Jason prayed.

It was my turn. "Lord, thank You for my family! And please don't forget to show Sara You love her! Amen."

"Before you leave the table, I have something to tell you," Dad said. "Jason and Katie, how would you like to go with us to the hospital?"

"You mean when Mom has the baby?" Jason asked.

I looked at Mom. She was smiling a huge smile! "Can we?" I asked.

"Why not?" Mom said. "You're both old enough. We thought you'd like to be there to welcome your little brother or sister yourself!"

"Yeah!" I was jumping up and down. "I can't wait!"

"There's just one problem," Jason said. "Who

will take care of January?"

Dad smiled. "It's OK, Son. It's all arranged. The Upjohns are going to pick him up this evening."

"From now on, all of you had better stick near the house," Mom said. "We might have to leave for the hospital at any time!"

A Midnight Ride

"Katie! Wake up!"

I was right in the middle of a dream. I was a fairy princess with red hair! A handsome prince was rescuing me! And the whole time this was happening, Sara was standing there saying, "See, Katie! I told you so!"

"Katie!" Dad was saying, "Are you awake?"

Suddenly, I sat up in bed. Although my father had turned on my light, I could tell that it was still dark outside. "Is something wrong? What's happening?"

Dad was smiling, and I could tell he was excited. "Katie, get dressed as fast as you can! This is it! The baby is coming! We have to get to the hospital!" And then he left my room.

Now, you better believe I was wide awake! I grabbed my jeans and started to pull them on over my pajamas. That's when I remembered what Sara said. Did I want my new brother or sister to see me looking like this? Of course not!

On the other hand, it felt downright stupid to be putting on a dress in the middle of the night! Which is why I stood, paralyzed, in the middle of my floor.

"Come on, Katie!" Jason was saying. "What's wrong? If you don't hurry, they're going to leave without us!"

"I don't know what to wear," I said.

"Don't be dumb!" my brother said. "We're just the siblings! Nobody's going to be paying any attention to us!"

"Don't call me names!" I said.

Jason laughed. "That's just what they call brothers and sisters!" He waited while I pulled on jeans and ran my fingers through my hair.

At the top of the stairs, we met Mom. She was carrying a small suitcase.

"Let me take that," Jason said. "How are you feeling?"

"Ready," Mom smiled. "I'm ready."

"Where's Dad?" I asked.

"I don't know," Mom said.

Everything about the dark house looked funny. It even *sounded* funny. Going downstairs caused a chorus of squeals and groans from the old floorboards.

"What time is it?" I asked.

"About one o'clock," Jason said.

"Mom, is it a rule that babies have to be born in the middle of the night?" I asked.

"I don't think so," she said. She stopped talking and hung on to the banister.

"Mom, what's wrong?" Jason asked.

"It's a contraction."

"Oh, no!" Jason said. "Dad!"

"I'm all right," Mom said. "This is what we've been waiting for!"

When we got to the kitchen, Dad was waiting for us.

"I thought you probably were boiling water," Jason said.

Dad took one look at him and started to laugh. "Don't be silly, Jason," he said. "I don't know why they always used to do that! I can't imagine what they ever did with it!"

Mom smiled. "Maybe it was just to keep the fathers busy!" she laughed. "Are you ready?"

"Let's go!" Dad said.

We locked the back door and started down the path toward Purple Jeep. Jason, still carrying Mom's suitcase, led the way with a flashlight. Dad walked next to Mom. I was last.

"This reminds me of the night we came out

here to look for our ghost!" I said.

Mom giggled. "That was fun, wasn't it!"

"Kids, your mother is the best sport in the whole world!" Dad said.

After helping Mom into her seat and tucking a blanket around her, Dad took his place behind the wheel. "Isn't this exciting!"

"Dad, let's go!" Jason said. "We don't have all night!"

As Dad turned the car around, he accidentally touched the horn. *Mary had a little lamb* sang Purple Jeep!

"Oh, no," Jason said. "You'll wake up the entire neighborhood!"

Dad just laughed. "Shout it from the rooftops! Let the whole world know! I'm going to be a father!"

"And I'm going to be a mother!"

"And I'm going to be a sister!"

We waited. Finally, Jason said, "And I'm going to be a brother!"

Everybody cheered!

"I'm just as excited as you are," Jason told us. "But I would have waited until morning!"

And then the Hooper family headed off to Colorado Springs to the hospital! I couldn't imagine being sleepy! Even before Dad turned onto the highway, we were wired! And with each turn of the road, our excitement grew!

"How did you know the baby was coming?" I asked.

"He called us long-distance," Dad said. "Didn't you hear the phone ring?"

"Dad!" I said. He just laughed.

"As soon as the baby can't get enough food and oxygen from the placenta and umbilical cord, he has to escape!" Mom said.

"And you can feel it happening?" I asked.

"I can," Mom said. "The process of being born is called *labor.*"

"Is that why contractions are sometimes called *labor pains?*" Jason asked.

"Right," Mom said. "The muscles of the uterus tighten up and then let go. It's kind of like making a fist with your hand and then releasing it. The force sends the baby down through the pelvis. The passages slowly widen and the infant comes out!"

"At first the contractions are far apart," Dad told us. "As birth approaches, they get closer and closer together."

"First babies usually take the longest," Mom said. "Babies born after that come quicker."

"Oh, boy!" Jason said. "I hope we make it to the hospital!"

"Don't worry!" Mom said. "My contractions are still far apart. The time between contractions has to get down to less than three minutes before the baby is born."

"Well, at least we don't have to worry about traffic," Jason said.

He was right about that! During the drive down Ute Pass, we didn't meet a single car! As we swished around the curves, my ears popped!

Now we could see the lights of Colorado Springs. "It's beautiful at night, isn't it?" Mom said.

"It's pretty now," Dad said. "But I'm glad I don't have to fight the traffic every day!"

As we pulled up to a stoplight, we were the only car at the intersection! "Maybe this is why babies like to be born at night," Mom said. "Less traffic!" She laughed.

"Mom, how far apart are the contractions now?" Jason asked.

"Don't worry, Jason," she said. "I'll tell you when the next one comes."

Even without traffic, it seemed like forever as we drove through the deserted streets. Now nobody was talking. I tried to watch for the hospital, but then my eyes started closing.

Suddenly, I heard Dad groan. "Oh, no! I can't believe it! I think I'm lost! Watch for a policeman!"

"Steve, don't get upset!" Mom said. "This is Academy Boulevard! Just keep driving!"

"It looks different at night," Dad said.

"Maybe it just looks different when you're going to have a baby!" Jason said.

"You're right, both of you!" Dad laughed. "There it is! There's the hospital!"

I was wide awake again! I watched Dad turn into the parking lot. Then I watched as he drove right past the entrance!

"Do people having babies have to go in a special door?" I asked.

"Not just a special door!" Mom said. "Katie, wait until you see this! It's a brand-new section of the hospital!"

We passed a lighted sign that said *Emergency* and another that said *Birth Center.* And then Dad was parking Purple Jeep across from the Birth Center entrance. We had arrived!

Through
the Glass Door

"OK, this is it!" Dad said. "Is anybody getting excited?" It was impossible to miss the excitement in his own voice! He leaned over and kissed Mom.

"I love you!" Mom said. "You, too, Katie and Jason! By the way, I just had another contraction!"

"How far apart were they?" Jason asked.

Mom laughed. "Can you believe it? I forgot to look at my watch the last time!"

We all laughed, too. We could believe it! Mom has absolutely no concept of time! Jason nearly dies every week while we wait for her to get ready for church!

My brother and I climbed out of Purple Jeep

and stood there in the dark while Dad came around to help Mom. As we walked across to the Birth Center, it felt like another family adventure!

Suddenly, like magic, the big glass door slid open, and we all walked through.

"I'm Steve Hooper," Dad told the woman at the desk. "And this is my wife, Elizabeth."

The woman wearing a red tie smiled at us. "Welcome to Penrose Birth Center!" she said. She checked something on her desk. "It looks like I have all the information we need, Mr. and Mrs. Hooper. And your room is all ready!"

Dad turned to us. "These are our children, Jason and Katie. For now, they're going to wait for us out here."

"Hi, Jason! Hi, Katie! We're glad you came along! As soon as I get your parents into their room, I'll be back to show you where you can wait."

"I guess it's good-bye for a little while," Dad told us. "I'll be staying right with your mother. But I'll try to come out from time to time to let you know what's happening." He smiled.

"Try to get some rest," Mom said. "It could be several hours before you can meet your little brother or sister."

I hated to see Mom and Dad go. "Family hug?" I said.

We all stood in a circle and hugged each other one last time. It's something we've done as long as I can remember.

"Next time we do this, I won't take up so much room!" Mom laughed.

We watched our parents disappear through a door on the left. "I feel kind of like I'm dreaming," I told Jason.

"Me, too," he said.

The woman returned. "OK, Jason and Katie, just follow me." She led the way into a beautiful room across the hall. "I'll bet you're excited!"

"That's for sure!" I said. "Are there any other babies here?" The waiting room was empty.

"Quite a few!" she said. "We have room for fourteen families in the new Birth Center. And last night all of the rooms were full!"

"How come there's nobody else waiting?" I asked.

"The other fathers are all in the rooms with the mothers—just like your dad."

"You know what?" I told her. "I've never seen such a pretty room! Never in my life."

"That wasn't very cool," my brother said, afterwards.

"It's the truth," I said. "The carpet looks like gray velvet. And I love the pink furniture!"

"That color isn't called pink," Jason said. "It has another name."

"Whatever." I glanced around. "What's that?"

"It's a fireplace."

"Are you sure? It doesn't look like one!"

"Oh boy! Take a look at that television!" Jason said. "I didn't know they came that big!"

"Well, I knew it," I said. I started to tell him about Sara's TV, but then I decided not to. With my luck, I'd be blabbing out her secret in the next sentence!

"I guess we might as well try to sleep." My brother kind of folded himself onto the closest chair and closed his eyes. "I wonder what time they turn it on?" he muttered.

"I'll sit over here," I said. But I don't think he even heard me.

The next thing I knew, Dad was standing over me again! "Jason, Katie!" he was saying.

"I'm awake," I said.

"Is our baby here?" Jason asked. "Has our baby been born?"

Dad shook his head. "Not yet. But everything's right on schedule. By the way, your mom's incredible!"

"Did you leave her alone?" I asked.

"The doctor's in there," Dad said. "And the nurses are setting up the room. We decided I have time to take you to the cafeteria for a quick breakfast."

"Let's go!" Jason stood up.

Actually, it turned out that Jason was the only one with an appetite. He ate three eggs! I was so excited I could hardly swallow my cereal. And Dad ... well, he even left his toast!

"You're sure Mom's all right?" I asked.

"I'm sure," he said. "She's telling everybody she feels like a queen! In fact, she keeps teasing me that she's never going home! Wait until you see our room!"

"What's that on your arm?" Jason asked.

Dad looked down. "It's my identification. They banded us when we first came in last night. I'll need this to get into the nursery."

"Was that the nursery we passed on the way to the cafeteria?" I asked.

"That's it!" Dad said. "Maybe you'd like to watch the babies when we go back."

"Can we?" I asked. Now I could hardly drink my orange juice.

"Just don't wander off!" Dad said. "I don't want to have to go looking for you!"

When Dad hurried back to Mom, he left Jason and me standing by the nursery window. "Ooooo!" I said. "Aren't the babies cute! Look at them!"

"I still think they all look alike," Jason said.

"Some don't have any clothes on! I wonder why."

"See the baby over there?" Jason pointed. "I

wonder if he's all right? Does it look like he's breathing funny?"

"You're imagining things!" I said. "Isn't it hard to realize we were once that small?"

"It's almost harder to realize that we're going to take a baby home with us!"

I looked at my brother. "Be honest," I said. "Are you hoping for a boy?"

"I don't know. I'm so much older that I honestly don't think it makes much difference," he said.

"Good," I said. "Then you can pray for a girl!"

Jason didn't say anything. He just stood there watching the babies. "You know, Katie, I was just thinking about all the things a baby has to learn to do after he's born!"

"You mean like walking and reading and tying his shoes?"

"Well, those things, too," he said. "But right off the bat a baby suddenly has to breathe for himself, and eat for himself—basic things like that!"

"It's a tough life!" I laughed.

"I'm going back to the waiting room," he said. "Are you coming?"

I shook my head. "I'll be there in a minute."

I don't know how long I stood there. I just couldn't take my eyes off those little plastic cribs!

I looked at all the little heads. Some of them

hardly seemed to have fuzz on top. But one baby had so much black hair you could comb it!

Then, while I watched, one baby started to cry! I couldn't hear it through the glass, but I could see him. I realized that before he was born, the baby never even cried! Suddenly, I began to understand what Jason was talking about!

Our Long Wait
Is Over

When I got back to the waiting room, Jason was glued to the television set. He hardly looked up when I walked into the room.

"What are you watching?"

"I don't know the name of it," he grunted.

"Why does that man look like that?"

"How should I know!"

"Is that a bad guy?"

Jason looked up. "Katie, be still! If you keep talking, I'll never figure it out!"

"Hi!" said a small voice.

I looked down. "Hi!" I said. "I didn't know you were here."

The sober little girl looked at me with big eyes. "Want to play?"

"Sure." I followed her into the playroom next to where we had been waiting. "What's your name?"

She just looked at me. I sat down on the floor next to her. "How old are you?"

She hugged her blanket. "Three."

"You're three!" I said. "That's wonderful!"

"My mom's getting a new baby!"

"She is?" I said. "That's wonderful!"

"I'm the big sister."

"Is that right?" I grinned. "You know what? I'm going to be a big sister, too!"

She didn't seem impressed. "My mom's getting a boy!"

"Well," I told her, "she *might* be getting a boy! Maybe you'll get a girl!"

"No! We're getting a boy!" She picked up a doll, hugged it, then threw it on the floor.

"Don't do that!" I said. "You'll hurt your baby." I picked up the doll and cuddled it. "Nice baby."

"I want my daddy!"

"Your daddy's busy right now," I said. "Pretty soon he'll come and tell you about your baby."

She just looked at me. After a few minutes, she came over and took her doll back.

I felt like cheering. "That's nice," I said. "Are you going to be a mommy when you grow up?"

"No," she said firmly. "I'm going to be an electrical engineer!"

I couldn't believe it. Frankly, I don't really know what an electrical engineer does! "Maybe you'll change your mind," I said.

The little girl wasn't listening. She carefully arranged her blanket in the corner and curled up with her doll in her arms.

Back in the waiting room, my brother was watching a game show. Whenever anyone gave an answer, everybody laughed.

"I think I'll go back and watch the babies," I said.

But just as I started out, Dad appeared in the doorway! He was grinning like a jack-o'-lantern.

"Jason! Dad's here!"

"Hey, kids, I have some wonderful news!" He paused.

"Tell us!" I begged.

"The Lord has given us a beautiful baby girl!"

It's a girl! I'm not sure what I did first! I just know that I was squealing and jumping up and down and hugging everybody. And Jason was telling me to quiet down. But I noticed that his smile was just as big as mine!

The little girl in the next room wandered out, still wide-eyed and serious. "I'm a big sister!" I yelled. "We have a baby girl!"

"Well, *I'm* getting a boy!" she said. Never once smiling, she turned and went back into the play-room.

"Can we see the baby?" Jason asked.

"She and your mother are waiting for you!" Dad said. "Let's go!"

As we passed the desk, Jason told the woman sitting there that we got a girl. Actually, it was a different person with a red tie. But she smiled anyway and said, "Congratulations!"

"We're in the third room on the left," Dad said.

As we walked down the hall, I really couldn't even feel my feet! I felt like I was floating!

"Come on in!" Mom said softly. She was propped up with pillows on a bed. I don't think I've ever seen her look so happy! And in her arms she was holding our baby sister!

"Jason and Katie, here's our newest miracle! Say 'hello' to Amy Elizabeth Hooper!" Then she looked down. "Open your eyes, Darling! It's time for you to meet the rest of the family!"

"Amy Hooper," I said. "It's a wonderful name!"

"And she's a wonderful baby!" Dad said proudly. He reached down and gathered her into his arms. "I love you, little Amy!" With his huge hands, he rocked and patted the tiny bundle.

"Your father was the first one to hold her," Mom said.

"Right after Amy was born, they laid her on your mom's stomach!" Dad said. "But as soon as they dried her off, they handed her to me!"

"How about a turn for Jason," Mom suggested.

My brother sat down on a chair next to Mom's bed. "I'm not sure I remember how to do this!" he said. "It's a long time since I held Katie!"

"You held me like this?" I asked.

Jason didn't answer. He was too busy cuddling Amy. "Hi, little sister! What a beautiful face! You've got to be the prettiest baby I've ever seen!"

"We told you they're all different!" Mom laughed. "Who do you think she looks like?"

"I don't know. Look at that little nose! This child is incredible!" He held Amy close. We watched while he rocked and hummed. Then he looked up at me and smiled. "Your turn, Katie!"

It was the moment I've been waiting for!

To be honest, I think it was the first time I've ever held a real baby, but somehow I knew exactly how to do it! I cradled Amy's fuzzy little head in my left arm and stroked her bright pink cheek with my right hand.

Suddenly, Amy opened her eyes! And she looked right at me! My heart *melted!* I can't even tell you how much I love her! When she closed her eyes again, I started to sing. "Hush little baby, don't you cry! Katie's gonna sing you a lullaby!"

"I didn't know you knew that!" Mom said.

I looked up at her. "I didn't know I knew it either!" I said.

I think that's when Dad started humming our praise song. And we all joined in. "Praise God, from whom all blessings flow; Praise Him, all creatures here below ..."

I looked up when a nurse stopped in the doorway and smiled at us. "Praise the Lord!" she said.

"I think this might be a good time to tell Amy her special Bible verse," Mom said. "What do you think, Steve?"

He nodded. "Katie, could I hold her for a minute?"

Amy opened her eyes and looked right at Dad.

"Amy Elizabeth Hooper," Dad said, "we praise God for your safe arrival!"

"She's listening," I said. "Look at her!"

Dad smiled and continued. "Amy, every child the Lord brings into our home is given his or her very own verse. Amy, you'll be hearing these words a lot! And before long, you'll be able to say them all by yourself!"

As Dad spoke, I thought of Psalm 16:11, my own verse. I realized that what my father said was true. I feel as if I've always known it!

Now we all listened as Dad spoke Amy's special words from God:

"Delight yourself in the Lord and he will give you the desires of your heart. Psalm 37:4."

"It's a perfect verse for Amy!" Jason said.

Mom smiled at Dad. "Picking the baby's verse is the first thing we do when we know we'll be having a baby," she said.

"I didn't know that!" I said.

Suddenly, Amy Elizabeth Hooper started to cry!

"I wondered if she knew how to do that!" Jason laughed.

"She's quite a genius," Dad said. "She learned that right away!" He kissed Amy and handed her back to Mom. "Now let's see if she knows how to eat!"

Our Family Time Continues

Mom arranged her hospital gown and held Amy to her breast. We all watched, fascinated, as the tiny mouth began to suck.

After a few minutes, Mom looked at us and smiled. "Well, I can see that Amy's eating isn't going to be a problem!"

"I don't understand how she knows how to nurse!" Jason said.

"Maybe the Lord sent her to baby school!" I laughed.

When Amy fell asleep, Mom laid her down on the bed. "I think it's time we all got a better look at her!" She gently unwrapped the small blankets. "Oh, look at those plump little legs and arms!"

"You can tell that she wasn't born early!" Dad said.

"How much does she weigh?" Jason asked.

"The scales are in the nursery," Mom said. "Amy hasn't been out of this room since she was born."

"You mean nobody's weighed her yet?" Jason asked.

"I'll be taking her over to the nursery when our family time is over," Dad explained. "That's when the medical team will weigh her and give her a complete examination."

"Look at those darling little feet!" I said. "Can I touch them?" I held Amy's legs in my hands and counted her toes.

"I hope you got to ten!" Dad laughed.

"I'd better do the fingers," Jason grinned. "You can't count that high!"

"You just want to touch them!" I said. And Jason didn't deny it.

"I can't believe those tiny fingernails!" he said.

"We don't want her to get cold!" Mom said. "I think I'd better cover her back up." But first, Mom rolled Amy over on her stomach so we could see her little back.

"Amy's definitely our biggest baby!" Dad said. "How much do you think she weighs?"

"Let's have a guessing contest!" Mom said. "I'll

go first. I think she weighs seven pounds, eight ounces. What's your guess, Jason?"

"I haven't any idea what the average baby weighs," he said.

"This isn't a mathematical problem!" Dad laughed. "Just take a guess, Jason!"

"OK. I'll guess seven pounds, seven ounces," Jason said. "A baby's mother can probably tell pretty close."

Jason had a good point. "Then I'll guess seven pounds, nine ounces," I said.

Dad laughed. "Amy's bigger than that, you guys! Did you see that fat little body! I say she's over eight pounds! Eight pounds, two ounces, to be exact!" He lifted her from the bed and pretended to be judging her weight. "I'll change that to eight pounds, three ounces."

"Are you sure?" Mom laughed.

"There's only one way to be sure!" Dad said.

"Before you take her away, haven't you forgotten something?" Mom asked. She smiled at Jason and me. "While we're all here together, we want to start teaching Amy Hooper about family hugs!"

"That's right!" Dad said. "Come on over on this side of the bed, Jason." Dad held Amy, and we all crowded up next to Mom.

Actually, it was kind of tricky, with Mom in bed and everything. But somehow we managed to have a wonderful family hug anyway!

"I'm so proud of my family!" Dad said.

"And we love you all so much!" Mom said.

Well, it was the best family hug in my entire life! While we were all bunched together, little Amy woke up. I'm sure she must have seen that we were all smiling! But I wonder if she noticed that Mom even had tears in her eyes!

"Well, I guess it's time for me to carry our third child into the nursery," Dad said. "Want to come with me, Jason?"

My brother smiled and nodded.

"Katie, why don't you stay here with me?" Mom said. "If all of you go, I'm going to get lonesome!"

When they reached the doorway, Dad turned and held Amy so we could see her one last time.

"Bye, Amy!" Mom called.

"Good-bye, Little Sister!" I said.

"Oh, my! Hasn't this been a special time!" Mom said. "Not all hospitals let families do this! It's the main reason we decided to have our baby at Penrose Birth Center!"

"Could you have a baby at home?" I asked.

"Some mothers do," she said. "But I like the idea of being in a hospital in case there might be problems. Behind those doors they've hidden all the equipment needed in case of an emergency."

"Amy was born right in this room?" I asked.

Mom nodded. "That's special, too! I'll be in this same room the whole time I'm here!"

For the first time, I really looked around. Frankly, it looked like a picture in a magazine! The colors were the same as in the waiting room. And everything matched! Even the wallpaper!

"The fathers can sleep on the window seat," Mom said. "Tonight we'll be having a celebration dinner at the table! And guess what's hidden inside there?"

"Can I look?" I pulled open the cabinet door and nearly fainted. It was a huge color television set!

"Are you going to watch it?" I asked.

"I might!" Mom laughed. "But that's not the biggest surprise! Take a look in my bathroom!"

I couldn't imagine a bigger surprise than a color TV. Actually, the Hoopers have never even had a little black and white set. Curious, I walked past Mom's bed into the bathroom.

What I saw was a bathtub so deep that a person would need a life preserver!

"Well, what do you think?" Mom was calling from her bed. "Every suite has its own jacuzzi! You can make the water churn like a river rapids!"

I went back into Mom's room. "Have you tried it?"

Mom laughed. "So far, I've been too busy! But you better believe I'm going to! By the way, did I tell you that I can have Amy stay here in this room with me?"

"Then that really *is* a crib!" I walked across the room to get a better look. I ran my fingers over the teddy bear decoration. "They certainly thought of everything, didn't they!"

"See that picture over the crib? Hidden behind it are things that might be needed in an emergency," Mom said. "For instance, there's oxygen—in case Amy might have trouble breathing!"

"Dad said you were teasing about staying here forever," I said. "Now I can see why!"

Mom laughed. "Katie, I couldn't afford to stay even if I got tempted!"

"When will you be coming home?"

"Tomorrow morning," Mom said. "Katie, the interesting thing is that the Birth Center just opened in June. I think the Lord had it ready to give us a special place to welcome Amy! But I mean it when I say there's no place like home!"

"I'm glad, Mom!" We smiled at each other.

"We're back!" Jason said.

From the smile on Dad's face, we could tell he had something to announce! "Wait until you hear this! Remember when I guessed Amy's weight at eight pounds, three ounces? Well, she's eight pounds, four ounces! Am I good, or what?"

"The greatest," Mom said.

"Guess what?" Jason said. "The nurse told us that fathers always guess the closest!"

"OK, Father! You win the prize!" Mom said. "It just happens to be a kiss from the mother!"

And Jason and I cheered as he bent down to collect.

Birthday Presents

Dad smiled at Mom. "Elizabeth, I think I'll drive Jason and Katie home now. Then while Amy is having her checkup in the nursery, you can get some sleep."

"That sounds wonderful!" Mom said. "I have an idea, Steve. When you call the Upjohns, why don't you ask if they can bring the kids back to the hospital tonight. Wouldn't it be fun to have Jason and Katie join us here for our celebration dinner!"

"Would you two like that?" Dad asked.

"Is it OK with the hospital?" Jason asked. My brother always follows the rules.

"They told us you're welcome to come!" Dad said. "Which do you want, steak or chicken?"

Everybody laughed. I knew everybody would choose steak!

"Don't forget to give them their gifts!" Mom said. "They're on my dresser!"

"Relax!" Dad told her. "I'll handle things! I want you to get some rest."

"Mom, don't worry about us. We'll be fine," Jason said.

After we took turns kissing Mom, we waved from the doorway. Then, while Dad telephoned, Jason and I went back into the waiting room. I wasn't surprised when Jason went over to watch the TV.

I looked for the serious little girl, but she was gone. The woman who had been watching after her was still behind the desk, so I went up to her to ask about the little girl.

"She's in the room with her parents," said the woman.

"Boy or girl?" I asked.

The clerk smiled. "The child was right. It was a boy!"

Dad came back and put his arm around me. "All set!" he said. "Let's go!"

The spell was broken. Without Mom, the ride home seemed downright lonely. Nobody said much. Mostly, I think everybody was tired.

Once we turned onto Route 24, Dad explained the plans. "I'm going to go back down to be with

Mom," he said. "You'll be OK alone today. This afternoon, Upjohns will drive you down for our dinner. They're going to wait and take you back home."

"Will we be alone tonight?" Jason asked.

"Mrs. Upjohn will stay with you," Dad said. "I'm going to sleep at the hospital. And at eight o'clock tomorrow morning, I'll bring Mom home."

"And Amy!" I said. "Don't forget Amy!"

"I won't forget Amy!" Dad promised.

When we got home, Sara was sitting on our back steps. "Well?" she said.

"We have a new member in our family," Dad told her. Then he looked at me and smiled.

"It's a girl," I said. "And her name is Amy Elizabeth Hooper."

"No kidding!" Sara said. "There really was a baby girl in there!"

"Can Sara come inside?" I asked.

"Not today," Dad said. "It isn't fair to ask Jason to be responsible. Sara, you can come to see Amy tomorrow morning!"

"How about Katie?" she asked. "Can I see her, too?"

Dad laughed. "Of course, Sara! If you hang around, you can probably see all of us!"

"See you tomorrow," I said. I watched Sara turn and walk slowly toward her house. And it was funny. Even though she has a huge TV at home, I felt kind of sorry for her!

A little later, Dad came downstairs with our presents from Mom. They were wrapped in pretty blue paper with ribbon and everything!

"How come *we* get presents on Amy's birthday?" I asked.

"Just enjoy them!" Dad laughed. "It probably will never happen again!"

I jerked the wrapping off and started to jump up and down! "Oh, wow!" I said. "I may not even come to the celebration dinner!"

Jason was just as happy! "This takes care of my time for the next few days!"

Dad smiled at us. "Mom will be glad to hear how much you like the books! But couldn't you look up long enough to say good-bye?" He laughed.

We put down our books and hugged him.

"Bye, Dad," I said. "I love you!"

"Tell Mom thanks!" Jason said.

"Tell her for me, too!" I said. "Four new books in my series! Oh, wow!"

As soon as Dad left, Jason and I curled up in the family room and began silently turning pages. We did rest, but mostly we spent the day reading. Actually, we read so long we had to hurry to dress up for the celebration dinner.

All the way down to the hospital, I listened to

Jason talk to Mr. Upjohn. I think he was trying hard to sound like a man. Frankly, it's the first I knew he cared about interest rates!

"The entrance to the Birth Center is around on the other side," Jason told Mr. Upjohn.

"The whole thing's brand new," I said. "You should see Mom's jacuzzi!"

"What I can't wait to see is that new baby!" Mrs. Upjohn smiled.

"Why don't you come in with us?" I said.

"Katie, I'm not sure if they can," Jason said. "I'll go ask at the desk."

"Thanks anyway, Jason, but we'll just wait until she gets home," Mrs. Upjohn said. "Besides, we planned to do some shopping in the Springs."

"It's very nice of you to drive us down," I said, as we got out of the car. "It's my first time in a Cadillac!"

Mr. Upjohn laughed real loud.

"Why'd you have to say that?" Jason asked, as we walked across the parking lot.

"It *is* very nice of them!" I said. "It's a long drive down here!"

"I meant the part about the Cadillac!"

"Oh," I said. "Well, it was the truth!"

"Not cool, Katie!"

"Oh," I said.

Inside at the desk there was *another* woman in a red tie. "I was wondering," I said. "Do you have to take turns with the red tie, or do you each have your own?"

She looked at me and laughed real hard. But she never answered my question.

Jason looked embarrassed. "Don't mind my sister!" he said. "May we please go back to the Hoopers' room?"

The clerk checked, smiled at me, and motioned to us to follow her.

"What's gotten into you?" Jason whispered.

When we got to our room, we stood in the doorway and looked in. Straight ahead was the little crib with Amy inside! Near the window seat, the table was set with a white tablecloth and a pink flower! Mom was all dressed, lying on her bedspread. And Dad was watching TV!

"Hi!" Jason said. "We're here!"

"Come on in!" Dad said.

For some reason, suddenly together again, we seemed like a totally different family! Maybe it was the fancy room. Or maybe it was because we were all dressed up like church. But everybody acted so polite. Even our voices sounded funny!

"I sure like my books," I said.

"Me, too," Jason said.

"I'm glad," Mom said.

"How was your ride down?" Dad said.

"Fine," Jason said.

"Did you get a good rest?" I said.

"I sure did," Mom said.

"Amy's in perfect health," Dad said.

"Wonderful!" I said.

"I'm looking forward to that steak!" Jason said.

"Me, too," Mom said.

"Same here," Dad said.

"Did you try the jacuzzi?" I said.

"I did," Mom said. "Twice."

I looked around. I felt shy. I couldn't think of one more thing to say! "I blew it!" I blurted out. "Jason said I wasn't cool! I told the Upjohns it was my first time in a Cadillac!"

Both Mom and Dad started laughing. "What did Mr. Upjohn say?" Dad asked.

"Nothing. But he sure laughed!"

"Just keep being yourself, Katie!" Mom said. "Being cool isn't everything!"

All of a sudden, everything was back to normal! Our family relaxed again. "Hey, sit down, kids," Dad said. "I want to tell you the neat thing that happened this afternoon. Amy's getting her picture in the newspaper!"

Amy's Homecoming

"I'm not sure I exactly understand it either," I told Sara the next morning. We were sitting on the back steps waiting for my parents to get home from the hospital.

"It doesn't make sense!" Sara said. "I mean, how can your sister get her picture in the paper just for being *born?*"

"It's not exactly for being born," I explained again. "It's because our family lives in Teller County. Dad says an awful lot of people are moving to our area!"

"I still don't see what that has to do with your baby," Sara said.

"You'll have to ask my father," I said. "Oh, here they come now!" As Purple Jeep pulled up along

118

side of the road, I opened our back door and called inside. "Jason! Mrs. Upjohn! They're here!"

We all ran out to greet Amy. "Welcome home!" Jason said.

Dad was grinning from ear to ear. To be honest, Mom looked really tired. But you could tell she was happy, too.

"Where is the baby?" Sara asked.

Mom turned around, and we all looked into the back seat. There sat Amy, all strapped into a little car seat!

"Where did you get that?" I asked.

"We rented it from the hospital," Dad said. "Since you were born, they made it a law in Colorado that babies riding in cars have to be strapped into car seats."

"Oh, Elizabeth! What a little doll!" Mrs. Upjohn said.

"Marty! Thanks for all your help!" Mom said. "Did everything go all right?"

"The children and I got along just fine!" Mrs. Upjohn said.

Dad climbed out and walked around to help Mom get out. "Want me to carry Amy in?"

Mom nodded. "Jason, will you please bring the suitcase?"

It was like a small parade. Dad, carrying Amy, led the way. Next came Mom, carrying the pink flower from the celebration dinner. Then came Jason, carrying the suitcase. I was next, carrying a diaper bag. At the end, Sara danced along beside Mrs. Upjohn.

"Aren't you excited?" Sara said. "I just have to tell you that I've never been this excited in my entire life!"

"I'm excited, too," Mrs. Upjohn said.

In the family room, Dad handed Amy to Mom. The rest of us formed a semicircle and watched.

"OK, Amy, we're home!" Mom said softly. "As soon as I get these things off, you can take a look around!" After she untied the ribbon, she removed Amy's little white hat. Next she gently eased off the tiny blue sweater. Then she turned Amy so we could see her better.

"Oh, Mrs. Hooper, she's so little!" Sara said.

Mom smiled. She laid the baby on her knees and pulled Amy's dress up so Mrs. Upjohn and Sara could see her legs. "I have to keep looking," Mom said. "I just can't believe I have such a plump baby!"

"See, Sara!" I said. "Isn't she beautiful! I told you she's the most wonderful baby in the whole wide world!"

"Katie, don't brag!" Jason said.

"It's all right, Jason," Mrs. Upjohn said, smiling. "Families are supposed to think their own children are wonderful!"

"Marty, would you like to hold her?" Mom asked.

"I was hoping you'd offer!" Mrs. Upjohn said. She sat down on the sofa, and Mom passed Amy over to her waiting arms. "Such a precious miracle!" She ran a finger across her cheek.

"Who do you think Amy looks like?" Sara asked. "It's hard to tell with her eyes closed."

"That's easy, Sara," Dad laughed. "She looks exactly like me! Especially the hair!"

Mrs. Upjohn stroked Amy's little head. "Well, Steve, could be!" After a few more minutes, she looked over at Mom and smiled. "Elizabeth, I'll bet Sara would like a turn!"

Sara's eyes got big. "Do you think I could?"

Mom smiled. "Just sit down here, Sara. Now curve your left arm—like this."

We all watched Mom lay our precious baby into the waiting arms of a girl we hardly know—a child with holes in the knees of her grubby jeans. I held my breath and prayed silently that Sara wouldn't drop her! I looked up at Jason, who was rolling his eyes.

Suddenly, Amy woke up.

"Well, hi, Amy Hooper!" Sara said. Then she looked up at Mom. "What do I do now?"

"You're doing fine, Sara!" Mom said. "Just keep on talking to her."

"Well, Amy, I was kind of hoping you'd have

red hair!" Sara said, in a shy little voice. She started to kind of rock back and forth. Her eyes never left Amy's face. "Amy Hooper, I wonder if you know how lucky you are? You have a big family. And everybody here already loves you!"

Amy just looked at her with those dark eyes. But a few minutes later, she began to cry.

Sara looked scared to death. "I didn't do anything! Honest, I didn't!"

"It's OK, Sara," Mom said. "She's probably just hungry. I was so rushed at the hospital. I didn't have time to finish feeding her before it was time to leave. Here, let me take her."

Mom reached over and picked up Amy. But the crying continued. My sister's face was getting as red as a beet. Mom rested Amy against her left shoulder and began to pat her little back. "There, there," she said. "It's all right."

Amy cried even harder. Suddenly, Mom started crying, too. Jason and I looked at each other; neither one of us knew what to do.

"I think Amy and I both need some rest," Mom said, as she tried to wipe the tears away. "I'm going to take her upstairs now."

Mrs. Upjohn stood up. "Let me help you, Elizabeth."

The rest of us watched as they left the room. Nobody said a word until Amy stopped screaming.

"What's happening?" Jason asked.

"Your mother is very tired," Dad explained. "Having a baby is wonderful, but it isn't easy! We're all going to have to give her a lot of love and understanding."

"I guess I'd better split," Sara said.

"Don't go," I said. "We could play backgammon on the back steps."

"I don't know how," Sara said.

"I'll teach you," Jason said.

Sara looked at me, but she didn't say anything.

"That sounds like a fine plan," Dad told us.

So Home Sweet Home settled down again. We didn't hear another peep out of Amy. And when Mrs. Upjohn came down later, she said Mom was sound asleep.

I have to say that the backgammon didn't work out as well. Although Jason tried his best, he never did get Sara to understand why she shouldn't string out her men all over the entire board.

"You'll never win!" Jason told her.

"Who cares?" Sara said.

Finally, my brother couldn't stand it any longer and left.

Sara looked at me and grinned. "Good," she said. "We're finally alone!"

Good News!

By late afternoon, Home Sweet Home was so calm it seemed as if Amy had always been part of the family. Mrs. Upjohn had gone home. Dad was upstairs painting a picture. Mom and Amy were asleep. And Jason had ridden his bike into town to see if he could buy a Colorado Springs newspaper.

"You don't have to help me, Sara," I said. "Setting the table for supper is my chore, not yours."

"You're sick of me! You want me to go home, don't you?" she said.

I just looked at her. "I didn't say that, Sara! I just don't want you to think you have to work all the time you're here!"

"It's really funny," Sara said. "Helping at your

124

house never seems like work!"

Jason was smiling from ear to ear when he walked into the kitchen. "I got a paper," he said. "Guess what? Amy's on the front page!"

I took one look at the picture and started jumping up and down.

"Quiet down, Katie!" Jason said. "You'll wake Mom and the baby! Let's go out on the back porch."

After I looked at the picture, I started to read what it said underneath.

"Here," Jason said, as he reached for the paper. "I'll read it out loud: 'Amy Hooper, newborn daughter of Stephen and Elizabeth Hooper, of Woodland Park, provides one more reason why Teller County has become the 26th fastest-growing area in the United States.'"

"Can I see it?" Sara asked.

"Sure. But please give it right back," Jason said. "I want to read the article."

Sara looked at Amy's picture. "That's really something!" she said. Slowly she handed the newspaper back to my brother.

Jason began where he left off. "It says here that Woodland Park has had a 44.8 percent population increase since the start of the decade."

"What does that mean?" Sara asked.

"It means that a lot of people have been moving here. It says that's why most of our streets aren't paved," Jason explained.

"But it isn't Amy's fault!" I said.

"Nobody's blaming Amy," Jason said. "They're just using her picture to illustrate what's happening here. She represents the population growth in Woodland Park."

When Jason went inside, he let us keep the newspaper. Now I studied Amy's picture more carefully. "Isn't she darling! It does look exactly like her," I said. "Don't you think so?"

Sara looked again. "If I didn't know it was Amy, I probably couldn't tell!" She grinned at me.

"That's just because she isn't your sister!" I said.

"I've been thinking," Sara said. "You know, it really isn't fair! After all, I'm the one who got the idea about getting my picture in the paper! And now Amy's getting all the publicity!"

"This doesn't mean your picture *won't* be in the paper," I said.

"It won't," she said.

"How do you know?"

"I just do," she said. "No matter what I do, they won't want my picture. And it isn't fair! I can never be a dog eating ice cream. And for sure I can't get born again!"

I looked at her. "Sure you can," I said.

Sara looked up. "Sure I can do what?"

"Be born again. Did you know that's in the Bible?" I asked.

"What are you talking about?"

"The Holy Bible," I said, slowly. "It's God's special book that tells us the things He wants us to know."

"I didn't know He wrote a book," she said.

"Well, He did. And Jesus says that *everyone* needs to get born again!" I told her.

"I don't get it!" she said.

"It happens when we trust Jesus to save us from our sins," I explained.

"What does that mean?"

I thought a minute. "Sara, remember when you said someone like God wouldn't listen to somebody like you?"

She nodded.

"Well," I continued, "none of us can ever make ourselves good enough to satisfy God! So we *all* need Someone to save us! My Sunday-school teacher has been teaching us all about it."

She was really listening. "Do you mean that I'm not the only one? Does *everybody* need to be rescued?" she asked.

"That's exactly what I mean!" I said. "And Someone already did it! His name is Jesus."

"I never knew that," she said.

We just sat there on the steps. I could feel my heart pounding. I took a big breath. I felt so excited I thought I'd probably never be able to say another word.

Sara's eyes were big. "Where did you find a copy of God's book?" she asked.

"Actually, we happen to have several Bibles in our house," I told her. "In fact, I even have one of my very own!"

"Wow!" she said.

"Come on! I'll get it and show you!"

"I can't," she said. "It's almost time for me to go home for dinner."

"Sara, that's what Sunday school is all about," I told her. "The teachers tell you what it says in God's Book." I smiled. "I'd really like it if you'd come with me. We could learn about Jesus together!"

She just sat there. "Well," she said finally, "to be honest, I was already thinking about it."

"Let me know," I said. "We leave here at 9:30."

Just then the back door opened. It was Mom, wearing her usual smile. "Girls, thanks for setting the table," she said.

"Is the baby all right?" Sara asked.

"Everybody's fine," Mom told us. "Including me! It's wonderful what a few hours sleep can do! Katie, I hate to break this up, but we're about ready to eat!"

Smiling, I stood in the doorway and watched Sara's red hair disappear.

Mom smiled and put her arm around me. "You look happy, Katie!"

"I've never felt happier!" I told her.

"Tell me about it later," Mom said. "We're ready to sit down and eat."

Another Kind of Birth

"Well," I said at supper, "guess who else might be having a birthday!"

I guess they didn't feel like guessing! Everybody just sat there and looked at me. Finally, Dad said, "Why don't you just go ahead and tell us, Katie."

"It's Sara," I said. "My friend, Sara Wilcox."

"I wish I had known," Mom said. "We'll have to pick up something for you to give her."

"You mean a person gets presents when she's born again?" I asked. "I didn't know that!"

Now everybody *really* looked at me! "Katie, what are you saying?" Mom asked.

"I told Sara Wilcox all about being born again," I said. "And I think she's interested."

"How did you happen to talk about that?" Dad asked.

"It's kind of a long story," I told them. "Do you want to hear it all?"

"Just give us the short version," Jason said.

"Well," I said, "it all started out when Sara wanted to get her picture in the newspaper."

"I can't believe it," Jason said.

"It's the truth!" I said.

"Go on!" Dad said.

"Well, when Amy got her picture in the paper, Sara was kind of jealous. See, she thought of it first!" I explained.

Jason groaned. "I'd hate to sit through the *long* version!"

"That's enough, Jason," Dad said. "Let Katie finish."

I took a deep breath. "I'm already skipping the parts about the tower of boxes and the parade," I said.

Even Mom looked at her watch.

"Anyhow," I continued, "on account of Amy's picture, Sara felt discouraged. She said she couldn't turn back into a baby and be born again."

"True," Jason said.

"Wrong!" I said. "I mean, that's when I told her that *everybody* needs to be born again! And she really listened. Deep down inside I just know she's going to become a Christian!"

Now I *really* had everybody's attention!

"Did you explain what sin is?" Jason asked.

"Well, not exactly," I said.

"I think Sara needs a lot of love," Mom said. "Did you tell her how much Jesus loves her?"

"Not today," I said.

"You probably should have just invited her to Sunday school," Jason said.

"I did. She's thinking about it." I was starting to feel awful.

"Katie, no offense, but you know how you always say the wrong thing!" Jason said. "Maybe you should let somebody else talk to Sara. Mrs. Upjohn said she's been taking a course in evangelism. I bet she'd do it!"

I looked around the table. "I thought you'd all be glad!"

"Katie, we are glad," Mom said slowly. "I guess we just want to be sure Sara understands what's involved."

"Wait a minute, everybody!" Dad said. "It sounds to me as if the Lord is already using Katie to tell Sara about Jesus! You don't need to be an adult with special training!"

"But not *Katie!*" Jason said.

"Yes, Katie!" Dad said firmly. "And, Jason, don't you ever doubt it!"

My brother looked down at his plate. Then he

looked at me. "I'm sorry," he said.

"God is creative!" Dad said. "He has His own special ways to reach out to every person! Being born again is just as much a miracle as being born the first time!"

Later on, during our prayer time, everybody prayed that the Lord would help Sara understand His Good News. And I started feeling wonderful again!

"Before you get up from the table, I want to show you something," Dad said. "I'll be right back."

He returned with a sketch in his hand. "Well," he said, as he held it up, "what do you think?"

"It has to be Amy!" I said. "Look at those bright eyes!"

"And those fat cheeks!" Mom said.

"And that bald head!" Jason laughed.

Dad grinned. "Actually, this was your idea, Katie! Until recently, I didn't realize how much your sketches meant to you!"

"They're my best treasure," I told him. "If the house catches on fire and burns down, that's what I'd try to save!"

Mom groaned. "Don't even talk like that, Katie!"

"I'm sorry, Mom! I just wanted Dad to know what they mean to me."

"I get the point!" Dad laughed. "Anyhow, I

figured Amy might like a set, too!"

Suddenly, I remembered Jason. "You don't have birthday sketches," I said. "Do you feel bad?"

"I really don't mind," Jason said. "I've always known you love me anyway!" He smiled at Dad.

"At your age, it's too late to start at the beginning," Dad said. "But I could begin making sketches on your birthday this year."

"You know what I'd really like?" Jason said. "Could you draw me sketches of both our homes? I'll always remember my life at the cabin!"

"I'll do it!" Dad promised. "I have to go up there anyway before Mayblossom McDuff moves in."

Jason really looked happy. Frankly, I'd really like a sketch of the cabin, also, but I felt as if I couldn't say so!

"By the way, there's something else we need to discuss," Mom said. "We haven't chosen Amy's symbol."

"That's right!" I said. "I got so excited at the hospital that I forgot all about it."

Getting your own symbol is one of the special things about being in our family! Every Hooper has one. We use them instead of our names when we write notes to each other. It's like a code.

For example, Mom's collected sheep since she was a girl, so her symbol is a lamb. Dad's symbol is a tree. I think it has something to do with Psalm 1. I have no idea why Jason's is a rainbow. Because I was born on Valentine's Day, my symbol is a heart.

"How do you decide on our symbols?" Jason asked.

"There's no special way," Dad laughed. "It isn't scientific!"

"We had two ideas for Amy," Mom said. "But we never did choose. Maybe you could help us."

"What are they?" Jason asked.

"I kind of liked the idea of a teddy bear," Mom said. "Especially if we had a girl!"

"Which we did," I said.

"And I thought somebody in the family should have a star!" Dad said.

"A star's easier to draw," Mom admitted. "And it might inspire Amy to get good grades!"

"Well, what do you kids think?" Dad asked.

"Teddy bear!" I said immediately.

Mom smiled. "Jason?"

"I think I prefer the teddy bear, too," he said. "It suits Amy." I was really surprised.

"Then that's what Amy's symbol will be!" Dad said. And on the corner of Amy's portrait, he drew the cutest teddy bear I've ever seen!

"I have an idea!" Mom said. "I think I could

stencil a row of bears around the top of the nursery walls!"

"Could you stencil hearts in my room?" I asked. "When we get it painted, I mean."

"I don't see why not!" Mom was enthusiastic.

"I guess we can save the star for our next baby!" Dad said.

"Oh, my!" Mom laughed. "Steve, I didn't know you were such a hard loser!"

"I can see it now," Dad grinned. "The headline in the newspaper will be: *A Star Is born!*" Dad laughed. "It's something to think about!"

"Not now," Mom said. "Definitely not now!"

We Meet Sara's Mother

Mom was upstairs nursing Amy when the telephone rang. "Guess what?" Jason said. "It's Mrs. Wilcox!"

"Who?" Mom asked.

"Mrs. Wilcox—Sara's mother!"

"I can't come now," Mom said. "Jason, can you take a message?"

Oh, no! Not Mrs. Wilcox! Not Mrs. Clean, whose home didn't have a water glass out of place! Then I remembered the Chinese Death Torture! And I realized that even the thought of meeting Sara's mother scared me half to death!

Once more, Jason called upstairs. "She wants to know if it's OK if she comes over in about half an hour," my brother said.

"That'll be fine," Mom told him.

"Can Dad and I still go to Upjohns to pick up January?" he called.

"No problem," Mom called back.

Suddenly, I realized that Sara's mother might not happen to like the fact that I told her daughter about Jesus! My only hope was that Mrs. Wilcox would forget about the Chinese Death Torture and just plain yell at me! "Mom," I said, "am I old enough to get persecuted?"

Mom didn't get the point. She just looked at me and laughed.

During the next half hour, I was so nervous that I actually picked up my room and made my bed! And when I heard the doorbell, I nearly fell down the last two stairs!

Mom answered the door. I heard Sara's voice saying, "Hi, Mrs. Hooper! This is my mother. I brought her over to see Amy!"

"Hi!" Mom said. "I'm Elizabeth Hooper."

"And I'm Karen Wilcox," Sara's mother said. "We brought a little gift for the baby."

I was never more surprised in my life! I'm not sure what I expected Mrs. Wilcox to look like. Probably a cross between Cinderella's ugly sister and the Wicked Witch of the West! Certainly I did not expect an ordinary, normal mother with straight blond hair and a friendly smile!

"You must be Katie," Mrs. Wilcox said.

I nodded. She seemed harmless enough, but you can't always tell.

"Katie, please take Sara and her mother into the family room," Mom smiled. "I'll go up and get Amy."

As we passed through our house, still piled high with moving boxes, all I could think of was Mrs. Wilcox's neat, uncluttered home! I felt very relieved when we finally got to the family room.

"So this is the haunted house!" Mrs. Wilcox looked around. "What a wonderful old home! Sara's certainly had a more exciting life since you took this place over!"

"This is the room with the secret passage," Sara said. "It's behind that fireplace!"

"Want to see it?" I asked.

"Not tonight," Mrs. Wilcox said. "We really can't stay. Katie, maybe you'd like to open this gift for your sister."

"Thank you," I said. I took it but decided to hold it on my lap.

Mom, with Amy in her arms, came down almost immediately. "I just fed her," she said. "She hasn't gone to sleep yet!"

"Ooooooh!" said Mrs. Wilcox. "It's hard to remember when Sara was that small!"

While the others looked at Amy's little hands and feet, I opened the present. "Look, Mom!" I said. "Her own little jogging shoes!"

Mrs. Wilcox laughed. "I just couldn't pass them by!"

"Mrs. Hooper, would it be all right if my mother held Amy?" Sara asked.

"Sara!" Mrs. Wilcox looked horrified. But when Mom carried Amy over and laid the baby in her arms, she smiled.

At first Mrs. Wilcox just touched Amy's cheek. Then she began to rock and hum "Rock-a-Bye-Baby." She seemed to forget that we were there.

Finally, Mrs. Wilcox looked up. "Thank you for sharing your baby!" she told Mom. "It brings back lots of memories. I always dreamed of having a big family. But when Sara was just a baby, my husband got very sick."

"You're alone now?" Mom's voice was soft.

Mrs. Wilcox nodded. "Sara's father was a wonderful man. But he couldn't handle his illness. He left us soon after Sara's first birthday."

I glanced over at Sara. Her eyes were open wide as she watched her mother speak.

"That must have been very hard," Mom said.

Mrs. Wilcox sighed. "It was hard," she said. "I wasn't employed. When my husband went away, I had to go back home to live with my mother. And several months later I heard that my husband died."

"My father's dead?" Sara asked.

Mrs. Wilcox stopped talking and looked over

at her daughter. "Sara, you know I told you all about your father years ago!" her mother said. "You've just never wanted to accept it!"

For a moment, Sara looked down at the floor. Then she looked up at her mother and smiled. "It's OK, Mom. I think I can handle it now," she said. "I just realized that I don't really need that fantasy any more!"

"I don't know what's happening to Sara," Mrs. Wilcox said. "When I got home tonight, it was like I came home to a different daughter!"

Mom looked at me and smiled.

"I told Mom I want to go to church with your family on Sunday," Sara said. "Mrs. Hooper, I hope it's OK."

"That would be wonderful, Sara!" Mom said. She looked at Sara's mother. "Karen, maybe you'd like to join us, too."

"Well, thanks for the invitation," Mrs. Wilcox said. "I don't usually work on Sunday mornings. And without Sara, my house might seem pretty lonely! I'll let you know. OK?"

At the door, I held my friend's hand. "Sara Wilcox, I love you!" I said.

"You know, Katie Hooper, I'm starting to believe that," she said.

"I really think God brought us both here to Woodland Park," I told her.

She grinned. "If you say so," she said.